SILENCING THE PEN

A ROGER AND BESS MYSTERY

M. LEE PRESCOTT

Silencing the Pen

A Roger and Bess Mystery

by
M. Lee Prescott

Published by Mt. Hope Press
Copyright 2023, M. Lee Prescott
Cover Design: Ashley Lopez
Image credit: istock.adobe.com/469163954
ISBN: 978-1-7379034-9-9 (print)

http://www.mleeprescott.com/

For my dear family, always!

CHAPTER 1

"All set?" he asked, watching Bess stuff legal pads into her canvas tote.

Dressed casually in gray slacks and a soft sage cashmere sweater, his wife wore a brightly colored scarf around her slender neck that picked up the color of her sky-blue eyes. Her light-brown hair was shoulder length and straight. Bess was five four with soft round curves, and Roger adored every inch of her.

Bess nodded, brushing a wisp of hair from her forehead. "Are you sure this is okay?"

Roger Demaris smiled, amazed every day that after decades of waiting, he now shared his life and his home, their beautiful home, with the love of his life. "I've lived on my own before, my love."

"That's not what I mean." She paused, hands on hips, blue eyes studying his. "The writing, the books. Harry's books."

He reached out, taking her soft hands in his. "You are my darling wife, and I couldn't say no even if I wanted to."

"Oh, Roger, you do mind!"

"I'm kidding, sweetheart." Surrounded by her sweet scent of citrus and jasmine, he smiled. A smile he reserved only for her. "I liked Harry, and you love the books, so why not carry on his legacy?"

"I'll probably be terrible at it."

He laughed, pulling her down on his lap. "No, you won't."

"I'm not a writer."

"Neither is Hillary," he said, referring to his second-in-command, Pete Dugan's live-in girlfriend. Roger headed RHD, a regional homicide unit based about twenty minutes from the village, and Pete was one of his full-time detectives.

He smoothed strands of hair from her face, kissing her temple. "I thought this is what this retreat was all about? Teaching you two and your fellow participants about the writer's craft?"

"Yes, for experienced writers!"

"That's not what the brochure you showed me said. I believe the words were 'beginners to experts.' Besides, you've been playing around with the manuscript for months. The parts I read were really good."

"Did they sound like Anne Greyson?" she asked, referring to the penname used by Harry Winthrop, her former fiancé, who had been murdered eighteen months ago.

Before his arrest for murder, Harry's editor had suggested that Bess might want to keep Harry's popular Anne Greyson books going. When Carrion Littlefield suggested it, she had laughed, but truth was she missed the mysteries featuring the intrepid Helen Brown and her faithful dog, Rosie. If she couldn't read any new stories about Helen, perhaps she could write them. After many discussions with friends and Roger, she finally decided, why not?

Littlefield was now serving a life sentence for his crimes, and his successor at the publishing house, Barbara Rollins, knew nothing about Bess's plans, but if the retreat went well, she intended to contact Barbara and set up a meeting.

"They're better than Anne."

She smiled, kissing him and running her fingers through his hair. Every month, a few more strands of gray appeared in the thick, dark mane. "Of course, you'd say that."

"Because it's true. If I'm not mistaken, your fellow author just pulled in the driveway."

"Oh, no! I'm not ready."

"I'll go. You finish up."

Bess stood as Roger opened the kitchen door and went down the steps to greet Hillary Dobbs. Except for her raven hair, his assistant's girlfriend could have been Pete's twin, with his same blue eyes, rosy cheeks, and freckles. He waved. "Hey, Hill. Come on up. She's almost ready."

HILLARY TOOK THE STONE STEPS TWO AT A TIME, GIVING HIM A HUG. "Morning, handsome." Pete's girlfriend had had a crush on his boss since the first time they'd met. She was a sucker for men with curly dark hair, and Roger's, now flecked with gray, was glorious.

Demaris's steel-blue eyes were arresting, whether they sparkled with warmth or blazed with anger. At five and a half inches, he was shorter than Hillary, with a barrel chest and broad shoulders. A few years earlier, he'd been stockier, but exercise and healthy eating habits since his heart attack had slimmed him down a bit. He was also well-educated and smart.

Hillary had discovered years earlier that Pete's boss had developed a carefully cultivated, crude manner of speaking, which he used to disarm and fool people. She had seen right through him. Hers was an innocent crush, shared by many who knew Roger Demaris. While people might find him gruff and abrupt, few could deny that the head of RHD had a presence, a strength, a command, that were obvious the moment he stepped into a room.

"I'm so excited. Is Bess?"

"Beside herself. Tough for Pete to let you go?"

She waved a dismissive hand. "He's glad to have me out of the house for a week. He gets to eat junk food, control the remote, and be a slob. Our monthly condo meeting is this morning, so he headed off before I did." Pete and Hillary lived at the Glen, a complex at the edge of town next to the river. "Only objection Mr. Junk Food made is that I'm using *our* vacation time to go away for a week without him. What he doesn't know is I've booked a ten-day island holiday for his birthday. Don't tell, Roger, promise?"

"Hɪ, ɢᴏᴏᴅ ᴍᴏʀɴɪɴɢ!" Bᴇss ᴄᴀʟʟᴇᴅ. "I ᴛʜɪɴᴋ I'ᴠᴇ ɢᴏᴛ ᴇᴠᴇʀʏᴛʜɪɴɢ!"

"Your laptop?" he said.

"By the door." Bess wheeled a suitcase, two bags slung over her shoulder.

"Here, I'll get those. Have you got snacks for the road?"

Hillary guffawed as she grabbed one of the canvas bags. "It's only a half hour to the ferry. I'm sure we'll survive."

All belongings stowed, Bess came round to give him a hug and kiss. "I love you," she whispered.

"Hey, not in front of the kids!" Hillary called as she hopped into the car.

"Me too, you," he said, gazing down at her.

"Miss you already," she said, burying her face in his neck.

"It's gonna be great. You'll be back before you know it with a terrific new book in hand."

"Optimistic, aren't you?"

"Always. Take care of yourself, and have fun."

As the women drove off in Hillary's mini Cooper, his heart constricted. For her sake, he loved that Bess was going, but he would miss her with every fiber of his being. He'd waited so long to be with her that even a minute apart seemed like forever.

CHAPTER 2

Bess smiled over at Hillary. "You ready for this?"

"I am. Can't wait! I was reading through the packet they sent, and we've got some huge names coming, don't we? I love Marilyn Lively's books."

Bess nodded. "Me too. Marilyn, Nancy Pratt, and Kyle Robles should make terrific workshop leaders."

"Do you like his books?"

"Honestly, not particularly," Bess said, as the car clattered over the wooden bridge crossing the river and out of Old Harbor. "Too dark and violent. I'm a cozy reader."

"And cozy writer!"

Bess laughed. "We'll see about that. I hope Harry isn't rolling over in his grave at my temerity." As soon as the words were out, she cringed. Somehow, her levity felt like a betrayal and affront to the memory of the man for whom she had cared very deeply.

"I'm sure he's smiling like the Cheshire cat. He'd be so pleased that you're carrying on with Anne Greyson."

"I hope so," she said, smiling. "Ferry turn-off a mile up on the right."

After a short ride on the "puddle jumper ferry," they landed at the docks of Gooseberry Island. As Hillary drove off the ferry, she sighed. "Beautiful, isn't it?"

Through the open windows, the scent of honeysuckle mingled with the sea air. On either side of the road, hydrangea, hibiscus, rose of Sharon, beach roses, sea grasses, Queen Anne's Lace and other colorful flowers bloomed, riotous and wild. There was a small general store near the dock and three small houses ringing the harbor, but otherwise the landscape was mostly undeveloped. Large tracts of the island were conservation land owned by SENCA, an organization which also owned much of its sister island, Winward, ten miles to the north.

"Yes, it's lovely," Bess said. "I haven't been out here since I was a child." She gazed up the hill spying the roof of the Gooseberry Inn. "And, then we only came for day trips."

"Pete and I came out for a few hours last summer to beach comb," Hillary said. "I've been begging him to come back and stay at the inn, but he says it's too quiet."

As they crested the hill, the inn came into full view. Punctuated by several towers and a half dozen chimneys, the enormous rambling Victorian stretched north and south along the hillside, its gray-shingled façade adorned with sea-glass-blue shutters. A wide wrap-around porch furnished with white rockers circled the entire building, affording magnificent views on all sides. Blue hydrangeas in full bloom grew under the porch, interspersed with lavender and black-eyed Susans. The property included a number of outbuildings —two large barns, several sheds, and two cottages. As they pulled into the clamshell drive, they spied a row of cars parked neatly beside the barn.

"We're not the first arrivals, I see," Hillary said as she pulled up beside a bright orange Land Rover.

"Hallelujah!" a voice called from the porch as Jane Fellows, Bess's dear friend and colleague at Old Harbor Friends School, jumped up from one of the rockers and came down to greet them. "Friends at last! I've been waiting for you!" Jane had arrived two nights earlier for "much needed R and R."

"Oh, Jane," Bess said, hugging her. "Are we crazy to be doing this?"

"Absolutely not! Although I will tell you that some people around here are taking themselves a little too seriously. Come on, let's get you settled. The opening workshop with Leo Tallstory begins in an hour."

"Tallstory?" Hillary said, pulling the bags from the back. "Are you kidding? Is that really his name?"

"Yup. He's a last-minute addition to the program. Very full of himself. Changed his name to attract readers. Thought they'd confuse him with a certain Russian novelist."

Bess laughed, eyeing her friend. "You're making this up, right?"

"Nope."

"I've never heard of him."

"Well, don't tell him that. He's a pretty popular writer of thrillers. He's only presenting today because Kyle Robles is coming a day late."

"But Kyle'll still be running workshops, right?" Hillary said.

"Cool your jets, sweetcakes," Jane said. "Mr. Gorgeous will be here for the whole rest of the week with his paramour, the lovely Fawn Davis."

"Never heard of her either," Bess said, following Jane into the inn.

"She's not a writer per se," Jane whispered, leading them to the reception desk and ringing the bell. "Fawn's a yoga instructor. She came early and will be offering daily classes. She told us yesterday that she may dabble with some poetry writing this week. She's also planning a nonfiction book at some point. In fact, here is the lady herself."

The reception desk sat in one of the inn's two parlors. As they waited, a tall, beautiful blonde in flowing caftan and black leggings strolled through the room. She was carrying a book and water bottle, her reading glasses pushed up, holding her waist-length hair back like a headband.

"Fawn, hi! Come meet my friends. I was just telling them about your fabulous yoga classes."

Davis's smile seemed forced. "Hello, welcome." The swirling

greens of her caftan reflected the deep green of her eyes. Empty eyes, devoid of light.

"Hello, so nice to meet you," Bess said, extending her hand, which Fawn ignored, bowing instead.

In the awkwardness that followed the woman's strange behavior, Hillary said. "I love yoga. When's your next class?"

"Six a.m. in the studio, just across the lawn in the barn. I'll leave you ladies to get checked in." After another slight bow, she disappeared.

"What was that about?" Hillary whispered.

"She's a bit affected, but she's a great yoga instructor. Just the right mix of gentle stretches and strengthening postures."

"Welcome to the Gooseberry Inn," a voice said behind them. They turned to find a rosy-cheeked woman, brown curls framing her freckled face. She appeared to be in her midtwenties, dressed casually in jeans and a purple Gooseberry Inn T-shirt. "I'm Clara Vickers. My parents own the inn. Can I get you checked in?"

"Do you live here, then?" Bess asked as the efficient young woman completed their registration and presented them with keys.

"I live in the private rooms right now. My parents have a small house down the hill, but we all live here during the warm months. In the west wing," she said, pointing to a closed door at the far end of the parlor. "You passed our house on the way. It's right near the ferry."

"What about the cottages out back?" Jane asked.

"They're rentals. Some people from your group are in one and the other's empty. My dad's been painting it. We have a very fussy client who comes next month. Thinks it's his exclusively, but it's not."

"It's a beautiful spot," Bess said, nodding as Clara handed her a key.

"For a week, but as a steady diet, maybe a little remote?" Hillary said, winking at the young woman.

Clara laughed. "Tell me about it. I've let Mom and Dad know that this is my last year. Here you go, Ms. Demaris, you're in 210, and Ms.

Dobbs, you're in 214, just down the hall. I'm sure Ms. Fellows can show you the way. I'll ask Matt or Henry to get your bags if you like?"

"Thanks, we can handle them." Bess accepted the key and a folder of materials. "I'm assuming no elevator?"

"Au contraire," Jane said.

Clara laughed. "Yup, we've entered the twenty-first century. Mom and Dad had it put in last year. It's around the corner, just before the door to the dining room."

CHAPTER 3

As they rode up in the elevator, Jane told them about the Vickerses' updates to the old inn. "They redesigned it as a retreat center, so they cut up the larger rooms and suites. Rooms have either a shared bath between adjacent rooms or their own bath. Some even have two baths because of the way things were broken up. It's very cool what they've done, even if they probably destroyed the historic integrity. From what they've told me, they're booked solid from March through November. It's one of the most sought-after retreat venues in the country."

"How many rooms?" Hillary held the elevator door as the others rolled the bags out.

"I think Clara said fifteen. Then there are the cottages."

"Who's staying in the one that's not under renovation?" Bess asked.

"Marilyn Lively and her husband, and their friend Nancy Pratt. As you know, Nancy and Marilyn are our fearless leaders. The cottage apparently has three bedrooms. Not sure if husband and wife are splitting up since they're on retreat and all. Here we are. This is your room, Hill. I believe you're sharing a bath with Jade and Ashlyn. They're together in one of the three double rooms. They're coauthors of those doggie mysteries."

"Oh, I love them!" Hillary said. "I think I'll unpack and take a short walk before the workshop. See you there?"

Bess smiled. "Yes, see you there."

Jane escorted her to her door and gave her a hug. "I'll let you settle in. I'm going to take a quick catnap. I'll knock on your door when I'm ready?"

"Perfect. I may follow Hillary's lead and take a quick stroll around the grounds to orient myself, but I'll be back in time."

BESS UNPACKED, THEN SLIPPED ON HER SNEAKERS, GRABBED A JACKET and her workshop materials, and headed downstairs. After asking Clara if she could leave her workshop folder and notebook at the desk, she headed to the entrance, checking her watch as she reached the front door. *A very short walk*, she told herself, as the workshop would begin in thirty minutes. The porch rockers looked very tempting, but she bypassed them and walked toward the cliff path that apparently ringed the entire island. The same riot of color greeted her as had on their drive from the ferry. Beach roses, wildflowers, and a tangle of goldenrod and Queen Anne's lace lined both sides of the grassy path.

Looking inland, she saw the two shingled cottages, a large barn where they would be taking yoga, and various sheds and a smaller ramshackle barn. As the field gave way to woods, she noticed what looked like an old pump house at the edge of the thicket and she wondered what life on Gooseberry Island had been like a century ago. The deep blue ocean below rippled with whitecaps, rolling waves crashing to the shore. Every so often, steps or dirt trails wound themselves down to the beach. The overgrown pathways and wooden staircases, tilted and broken, suggested that these passageways to the beach were seldom if ever used.

After ten minutes, she turned back, not wanting to be late for the workshop. As she gazed down at the water, she thought back over the past few years. First there was her emergence from ten years of grief for her first husband, Macomber Dore. Until charming, handsome Harry Winthrop came on the scene, she hadn't been able to let the memory of dear Mac go, but Harry swept her off her feet. Harry was dashing, but also kind and generous, to her surprise, Bess found herself falling in love with the son of the school's and village's biggest benefactor, Harry Winthrop Senior. Harry's murder had plunged her once again in a dark hole of grief, only to be rescued by Roger Demaris, her first love. High school sweethearts, the pair had broken up because of their life circumstances. Roger had made the decision and broke her heart because he didn't want to hold her back.

"There you are!" Jane called from the porch as Bess crossed the lawn. They walked in together and found two seats. When most of the group had assembled in the largest of the two front parlors, Nancy Pratt stood. Pretty, preppy, and petite, she wore her straight, shoulder-length dark hair pulled back with a tortoise band. She was dressed casually in gray linen slacks, a mauve top with three-quarter sleeves, and espadrilles, little or no makeup except for her bright red lipstick.

"Welcome everyone to the second Gooseberry Writers Retreat. So exciting to see familiar faces from last year. I look forward to hearing about your progress over the past twelve months. I hope everyone picked up your folder when you registered. If not, please see me after the workshop. In your packet, you'll find the week's schedule, your critique partners, and your appointments with the editors and agents who will be with us on Thursday. My codirector, Marilyn Lively, has not arrived yet, so I'll start us off. Marilyn and her husband, Beck Bailey, will be arriving tonight. We look forward to an amazing week.

"Might we start by asking each of you to introduce yourself, where you're from and your genre or genres. Please be brief as there'll be lots of time to get to know each other over the next five days, and we want to get right into our first workshop. I'll start. I'm Nancy Pratt from Boston, and I write romantic suspense." She waved to a couple on her right.

A diminutive woman in her late thirties or early forties sat up straight and cleared her throat. "Hello, I'm Wilma Conlon. I'm a

librarian from Northport. I'm working on a local history guide."
Dressed in green capris and a white T-shirt that hugged her plump
midriff, she styled her shoulder-length brown hair in a neat bob. Her
introduction completed, she nodded to the fifty-something man next
to her.

Well known to Bess and Jane, the man wore a green Franklin Fish
Company T-shirt and faded jeans. With deep blue eyes and rosy
cheeks, he surveyed the assemblage, nodding. "Bob Franklin, from
Mattapoisett. As an old fisherman, I'm toying with writing a mystery
set at sea." He then turned toward Fawn Davis to his right.

"Most of you know that I'm Fawn, Fawn Davis. My husband, Kyle,
and I are from Providence. He'll be here tomorrow. I'm writing a book
about mindfulness and maybe a little poetry."

The trio of Hillary, Jade, and Ashlyn went next. "Hillary Dobbs,
from Old Harbor. I'm lookin' to write a sassy, hot romance. So glad to
be here and lovin' my terrific fellow writers."

Ashlyn winked at her. "Back atcha, babe. I'm Ashlyn Fields. My
sister Jade and I are from Northport. We cowrite mysteries featuring
canine and feline sleuths. Have anything to add, sis?"

Jade smiled. "Nope, I think you covered it, Ash. Glad to be here!"

A study in contrasts, the sisters could not have been more different. Jade had curly sandy hair, wide brown eyes, and appeared
anorexically thin under her baggy sweats and long moss-colored
tunic-like sweater. Her smile seemed forced, and as soon as she
stopped speaking, it disappeared. Ashlyn's light brown hair was
straight, trailing down her back and shoulders, and her pale blue eyes
radiated warmth. Athletic and muscular, she wore faded jeans and a
casual jersey top.

Bess and Jane introduced themselves, then deferred to a gray-
haired older man to their right, who sat ramrod straight in his chair.
Bess had noticed him right away as there was something vaguely
familiar about him.

"Yorky Strauss," he said, nodding in her direction. "I'm also part
of the Northport contingent. I write mysteries."

Finally, a tall, slender woman with salt-and-pepper hair, gray linen slacks, and a plain white top, spoke. "I'm Claire Rubin from Marian. I join you as a true beginner. My hope is to write a children's book for my grandchildren." She gazed around the room, nodding at Bess and Jane. "So good to see some familiar faces."

As Claire fell silent, Nancy stood up. "Thank you, everyone! There are several more participants not present. Our hostess, Bella Vickers, who has already published several lovely romance novels, will be joining us, and of course, dear Kyle, and Marilyn Lively and her husband, Beck Bailey, all very accomplished, well-known writers. As I said, Marilyn and Beck should be arriving shortly.

"Without further ado, it gives me great pleasure to introduce our first speaker, this handsome devil by my side. Leo Tallstory has graciously agreed to step in for Kyle Robles, who was meant to run this first workshop. As I shared, Kyle has been unavoidably detained in New York City, but will join us tomorrow.

"Leo Tallstory is well known to everyone, I'm sure. As one of the country's most well-respected thriller authors, Leo has won a number of awards and been featured on many bestseller lists over the years. I will leave it to you to consult the bio of Leo in your packet for a detailed description of some of his many accomplishments. Please join me in giving a warm round of applause to Mr. Leo Tallstory."

The man himself swished to his feet, then waltzed to the podium. Tall and gangly, he had short, spiked salt-and-pepper hair, languid hazel eyes, and a perfectly trimmed goatee. In shiny gray vest, black pinstriped pants, and wingtips, he appeared to be auditioning for a role as a Victorian dandy.

Jane leaned over to Bess and whispered, "Who does he think he is?"

Bess nudged her. "Shush!"

With a slight bow, Tallstory clicked on his PowerPoint and began. "My fellow writers, I cannot tell you how enchanted I am to be here among you."

In his taut, staccato voice somehow reminiscent of Elmore Leonard's prose, he spent the next hour regaling them with stories of his own successes, but offered almost nothing about how he'd gotten there, his writing process, or the craft of writing. As Bess listened, she found little of interest and hoped they would not be seeing him at the podium again. Although Mr. Tallstory was listed as one of her critique group members, she breathed a sigh of relief to read that she'd been assigned Nancy Pratt as her expert critique partner. Nancy wrote romantic suspense and was certainly much nearer to Anne Greyson than Leo Tallstory or Kyle Robles, the other experienced mystery writers in the group.

CHAPTER 4

Bess and Jane were enjoying a delicious dinner with Hillary, her suitemates Jade and Ashlyn and Wilma Conlon, the librarian from Northport, when Leo Tallstory came by. He bowed, waving one arm in greeting. "Hello, ladies, just making the rounds."

"Mr. Tallstory, hello," Jane said. "Wonderful presentation, but you never told us the origins of your unusual name."

Bess gave her friend a sharp look. Jane had just spent the cocktail hour complaining about wasting her time in the opening workshop with "that bag of hot air."

"Join us, Leo," Ashlyn said, patting the empty chair beside her.

"Sorry, darling, duty calls. I'm just saying hello, getting acquainted with my fellow authors. Ms. Demaris, lovely to meet you." He gave Bess a dead-fish handshake. "I knew your Mr. Winston, you know. Talented writer, and what a sly fox he was, keeping his identity a secret for so long. I really enjoy the Anne Greyson books."

"Me too," Bess said.

"Harry's last name was *Winthrop*, Mr. Tallstory, not Winston," Jane said as she watched the color drain from her friend's face. While Bess was happy now and deeply in love with Roger, the circumstances of her fiancé's death still haunted her.

"Leo, please, Jane, dear. I feel like *we* are old friends already." With another bow, he moved on to the next table.

"What an ass," Jane whispered. "Old friends, indeed!"

As dessert and coffee were served, a flurry of activity at the dining room door heralded the arrival of Marilyn Lively and Beck Bailey. Bess recognized her right away from her book jackets. As in her photos, her lustrous auburn hair fell over her shoulders. Violet eyes scanned the room with nary a flicker of acknowledgment or recognition. In Bess's opinion, she was overdressed in her blue satin sheath, matching bolero jacket, and five-inch heels. Her husband was in khakis and a peach polo shirt, a navy sweater draped around his shoulders. His salt-and-pepper hair, longish and wavy, was thinning on top. Both in their late fifties or early sixties, he looked it, she didn't.

"The lady herself," Jane said. "At least she's a decent writer. Looks like she's come from a cocktail party."

Ashlyn sat back in her chair, staring, mouth agape. "Isn't she gorgeous. I can't believe we're going to be spending the week with her. I love her!"

Hillary smiled at her new friend, her blue eyes glued on the famous writer. "I know. I can't wait for her newest book. It comes out soon, and there was a rumor that she might be bringing advance copies this week."

"I've already got it on preorder," Jade said. "I reread all the books in the series every time a new one comes out. They're all on my iPad."

"Wow, you are a devoted fan, aren't you?" Bess said.

Her sister nodded. "There are literally thousands, maybe millions of us out there. Marilyn has more groupies than Danielle Steele or Nora Roberts, including Jadie and me."

"Can I bring you ladies anything else?" Angie, their waitress, asked as she cleared their dessert plates. Slender, with straight, sandy-blonde hair, the pretty young woman appeared to be in her early twenties. She gazed around at them, blue eyes warm. Waitstaff wore white shirts and black pants. Angie's appeared at least a size too big.

"Not for me, thanks," Bess said.

"How are you settling in? Ms. Demaris, isn't it?" Angie asked.

"Yes. I'm settling in beautifully. What a lovely spot this is. Have you worked here long?"

"My first summer. I heard about the job from Georgia." She pointed at the other waitress, who had long brown hair and was about her same age, who was chatting with Nancy Pratt. "We both go to Greenleaf," she added, referring to Greenleaf College, a small liberal arts college north of Old Harbor. "Love it here so far."

"What's not to love?" Jane said.

"Exactly," Angie said. "I'll just get these out of your way."

As she retreated, Jane said, "She's also one of the maids. She, Georgia, and Clara take care of the housekeeping in between meals. Seems like a real grind, poor things."

"As bad as the cruise ships," Ashlyn said. "Jadie and I did a writers retreat on one last year, and we got pretty friendly with the staff. They work 'em to death. Couldn't pay me a million bucks to do their jobs."

"But you do get to travel the world," Bess said.

"Fat lot you see of it when you're stuck far below deck twenty-four seven," Jane said. "Are we ready, ladies? Time to meet our critique partners."

After a lively evening with her mystery critique group, which consisted of Bob Franklin, Leo Tallstory, Nancy Pratt, Jade, Ashlyn, and Yorky Strauss, Bess met Jane in the front parlor, and they decided to take a walk before retiring. The sun was setting, but a full moon lit the wide path that circled the island. From every point, they could see the water, the moon reflected in its rippling surface. "Oh, this is lovely, isn't it?" Bess sighed.

Jane placed her arms around Bess's shoulders, hugging her. "You miss him. Admit it."

"Yes, I do. We... It's still so new, and I'm always a little afraid when we're apart."

"He's fine, sweetie. And he's got Pete the bulldog looking out for him."

Bess laughed. "Well, there is that."

CHAPTER 5

Later as they neared the inn's front doors, they heard shouting and spied two women on the east end of the porch. "Leave it alone, Daisy. Please!" the taller woman said.

As they drew closer, Bess recognized the tall woman, Fawn Davis, but not her companion. She looked over at Jane.

"The obnoxious, spoiled-rotten daughter. She works here, but also fancies herself a poet. You should've heard her drivel in tonight's group. Nasty piece of work if you ask me," she whispered. "Hello, Daisy, Fawn! Beautiful evening, isn't it?"

"Thank God Kyle's coming in the morning. At least I won't have to spend any more time with you!" Daisy said.

"Daisy, I was just telling Bess about your poems," Jane said, waylaying the petite young woman.

Daisy's hazel eyes flashed fire, hands on hips. Like her mother, she was dressed in yoga clothes, flowing black pants and long-sleeved top, the spandex a riot of swirling color. Unlike her mother, she was not a beauty. In fact, she was rather plain with a thin, pinched face, pale cheeks, and lifeless sandy-blonde hair tied back in a ragged ponytail.

"Now's probably not the best time," Fawn said, smiling apologetically at Jane.

Daisy turned her back on her mother, giving them her full attention. "Hi, Ms. Fellows. I enjoyed tonight's discussion, and I'm really looking forward to working with our critique group."

"Did you travel far to get here?" Bess asked.

"No, when I'm not at school, I live in Bell Haven, but the Vickerses have given me a job, so I get to stay all summer. They're hiring my boyfriend too."

Fawn's eyes registered surprise. "Scott? You didn't tell me that."

"My business. Mine and Scott's. Besides, when would I get a word in edgewise with all your lecturing?"

Jane looked over at Bess. "What jobs will you two be doing?"

Daisy shrugged. "Same as all the others—waiting on tables, housekeeping, gardening, whatever they need."

"Is your boyfriend here, then?" Jane asked.

"Not till Tuesday. He has a job in Bell Haven, but he's glad to quit. It's a crap job at Walmart. We plan to travel next fall."

Fawn shook her head, her placid expression now replaced by a scowl. "Ladies, I'm going to turn in. Will I see you at sunrise yoga?"

Bess smiled. "Count us in. Jane's been singing your praises."

"Just like the rest of the world," Daisy mumbled. "Fawn the perfect. Nighty night!" She skipped down the porch stairs and disappeared around the side of the inn.

Fawn sighed. "I'm so sorry you had to hear all that. We're not exactly on the best of terms at the moment."

They said their good nights, and Bess and Jane headed upstairs. They waved at Hillary, Jade, and Ashlyn, who were in the east parlor playing a board game. When they reached Bess's room, she turned to her friend. "Wanna come in?"

"No, thanks, I'm beat. Are you really up for yoga?"

"Absolutely. Please knock on my door on your way down. Night." She gave Jane a hug.

Once she'd slipped into bed, Bess grabbed her cell phone.

He answered on the first ring. "Hey."

"Hi. Miss me?"

"You have no idea. How's the retreat so far?"

"Interesting."

She gave him a brief description of the day. At the conclusion, he said, "Sounds like a lot of egos under the same roof. Watch yourself, my love."

"How was your day?"

"Quiet. Pete and I caught up on a mountain of reports. He, Brendan, and I had a bachelor dinner at the Tavern."

"Good. Now I know you're not starving."

They talked for a while longer, neither wanting to break the connection. Finally, she said, "Well, I'd better get to sleep. Jane and I are going to sunrise yoga."

"Lucky you. Take care of yourself, my darling."

"I will."

"Love you."

"Love you."

Bess held the phone for a few minutes after saying goodbye, then finally plugged it into its charger and turned out the light.

CHAPTER 6

Yoga was held in a beautiful studio space recently added to one of the property's barns. A wall of glass afforded views of the ocean, the opposite wall mirrored. Fawn taught gentle Kripalu yoga in the mornings and a more moderate class some afternoons. She also offered yoga dance several days at noon, according to the schedule.

"What a space," Bess said as they settled themselves on mats.

Jane nodded. "Spectacular, isn't it?"

Ten of them sat cross-legged on purple mats, surrounded by brightly colored woven blankets, and pillows. Fawn sat at the far end, with two mats crisscrossed under her. "Welcome, all," she said as she picked up a small book and read a Rumi poem in her soft, soothing voice. At its conclusion, she said, "Remember to listen to your own body and what it tells you. Our yoga is deepest when we listen to what we need and support ourselves completely with gentleness and love."

Gracefully, she led them through a series of flow practices for the next hour, ending in savasana, a deeply relaxing, restorative fifteen minutes lying covered with blankets. Beside her, Bess heard Leo Tall-story snoring. When Fawn called them gently to a seated position,

Wilma Conlon gave him a gentle poke, to no avail. Shrugging, she stood up.

"That was heavenly. Thank you, Fawn," Marilyn Lively said, waving on her way out, arm in arm with Nancy Pratt, who also called her thanks. Hillary, Jade, and Ashlyn stayed behind to chat with Fawn, while Yorky Strauss took a seat by the windows gazing out at the sea.

As Claire Rubin slipped out, she nodded at the two friends. "Bess, Jane, so good to see you."

They returned her greeting, then headed across the grass to the main building. As they stepped through the front door, they met Daisy coming out. She was dressed in shorts and a singlet, running shoes and socks in her hand. "Morning, Daisy," Jane said. "We missed you at yoga."

She scowled. "I don't do yoga. At least not when *she's* teaching it."

"It was a lovely way to start the day," Bess said, smiling at the young woman.

"I need a good hard run to wake me up. Oh, there you are," she said, nodding to Henry Lewis, one of the staff. A junior in college, Henry was tall and lean, with a head of tousled blond curls.

"Hey," he said. "All set, but we better hurry. I've gotta be back to serve breakfast."

"Me too," Daisy said as they waved over their shoulders. "See you soon, ladies!"

"So, she's gonna work, then put on her writer hat and join us, I guess," Jane said as they headed up to their rooms. "Busy little bee, isn't she?"

"Seems to be a very unhappy young woman at present," Bess said, unlocking her door. "Meet you at breakfast?"

"Good morning, ladies, I hope someone's taken your breakfast order? I'm Bella Vickers, owner of this place and your fellow workshop participant." Bella nudged strands of dark brown hair from her forehead. Dressed in jeans, a checkered shirt, and apron, her petite frame exuded energy.

"So good to meet you," Bess said. "What a beautiful spot you've created here."

Their hostess beamed. "Thank you. It was a beautiful spot long before Ron and I mucked about with it, but we like it. You must be Ms. Demaris."

"Bess, please."

"I'm Jane," her companion said. "We finally meet. Your husband and daughter have been most hospitable."

"I'm glad to hear that. I apologize for not finding you sooner. I've been out straight and off-island most of the past week, getting supplies for the retreat."

Jane smiled at her. "Don't know how you do it all and still have time to write those incredibly popular romances of yours."

"Well, my fans are not happy with me right now as I'm three months overdue for the newest Heather Island Romance. Sorry, must run. See you at this morning's workshop? Marilyn is super. Have you heard her before?"

They allowed as how they hadn't and waved as she flew off to direct the waitstaff, most of whom were chatting by the coffee station. As the boss approached, they scattered coffee urns in hand and Angie soon appeared at their table, asking if they needed refills of coffee or tea.

"All set, Angie," Jane said, looking up at the flustered young woman. Dark circles ringed her eyes, and she appeared to have rolled out of bed in her clothes from the previous evening. "Rough night?"

She grinned. "You could say that. I'm not exactly a morning person. I'll get my rhythm in a few days, though." When she smiled, Angela Smith was beautiful, her features seeming to fall into place. Even her bloodshot blue eyes sparkled.

"I'm sure you will, Angie, thanks, I'm all set with my tea too," Bess said.

CHAPTER 7

Marilyn Lively's workshop focused on writing believable, deeply human characters with whom readers would fall in love. The men looked slightly bored, except Bob Franklin, who hung on her every word. Daisy sat with Hillary, Jade, and Ashlyn. Jane and Bess shared a table with Claire Rubin, Yorky Strauss, and Bella.

That's what Harry did so well, Bess thought. The characters in the Anne Greyson mysteries lived and breathed with life, especially his sleuth, Helen Brown. *How will I ever come close to writing like that?*

Jane poked her, surreptitiously pointing across the room at a slumbering Leo Tallstory.

"Guess his nap during yoga wasn't enough," she whispered.

Bess suppressed a giggle, frowning at her friend.

During the question-and-answer period, Daisy raised her hand. "As you all know, I'm a poet, and I'm wondering how this relates to poetry. Is there a connection?"

"Absolutely," Marilyn said, waving her arms broadly. "Poetry is all about passion and life. The qualities that make poetry so powerful can be extraordinary when brought to one's prose."

"And this means?" Jane whispered.

"Hush!" Bess said, suppressing another giggle.

The session ended after a few more questions and Bess and Jane decided to take a walk before lunch. They headed for the footpath that hugged the cliffs. Bella had recommended it at breakfast, explaining that the seven-mile path ringed the entire island. As they reached the cliffs, the scent of the ocean mixed with the pungent fragrance of beach roses and pine surrounded them.

Bess sighed. "Beautiful. We should be writing out here. Talk about inspiration."

"Tell that to Marilyn. I'm sure the sea breezes would wreak havoc on her hairdo."

Bess chuckled. "Come on, my cynical friend."

Jane pointed ahead to a rocky outcropping in the distance. "Let's walk as far as the headland."

"Sounds good. So how are you doing? I haven't seen much of you in months."

"That's because you are in the throes of marital bliss."

Bess gave her a goofy smile. "I always have time for you."

"I'm fine. This retreat has been really helpful. I thought I'd concentrate on writing poems, but I'm actually thinking about a memoir. You know my childhood was kind of a nightmare. It might make a good book, or at least be a cathartic experience."

"Is that where your passion lies now, do you think?"

"Who knows? I'm still not recovered from the Thurbert debacle," she said, leaning on Bess's shoulder. Jane had carried on an affair of many years with the former headmaster of Old Harbor Friends, where both women taught, Bess as an art teacher, Jane, biology.

"I'm sorry about you and Peter. I bet he'd be happier with you than Carrie. She's kind of a cold fish."

"You don't know the half of it. She's still carrying on with Will, you know."

Bess stopped and stared at her friend. "Really?"

"Yup. Refuses to give him up. Says he's her lifeline. Nice, huh?"

"Poor Peter."

"Don't waste your energy on him. He could leave her now if he wanted to."

Bess glimpsed tears in Jane's lovely green eyes. "You loved him, didn't you?"

Jane brushed a tear from her cheek. "Still do. That's how pathetic I am."

Bess put her arm around Jane's shoulders as they continued to walk. "You are not pathetic in the slightest bit. Loving someone is very brave and hopeful."

Janie leaned over, resting her head on her shoulder. "You would know, dearie. You have certainly loved well. This is nothing against Mac or Harry. I loved them both, but I think you've finally found your true love. Your soul mate."

"He is that," Bess said, softly. "I just wish he... His job and all. I spend most of my days worrying if he'll come back to me."

"Roger? Count on it. Harry wasn't a cop, and look what happened to him. Mac... Well, Mac was different. Can't really dodge his kind of cancer."

"I'm seeing a therapist to try to deal with the fear."

"Good."

"We'd better go in," Bess said as they reached the inn's back porch.

"Let's try to avoid Leo. He has terrible breath."

The first people they spied on entering the dining room were Hillary, Jade, and Ashlyn. Hillary waved them over. "Sit with us. We saved two seats for you."

"Wouldn't you rather invite some of the younger people?" Bess asked, smiling at the three who had already become best friends. Hillary's dark hair was pulled back in a French braid, which Ashlyn appeared to have emulated. Jade was in yoga pants and a mauve tunic sweater. Her sister and coauthor was in jeans and a Bates College sweatshirt.

"No, we'd rather sit with the young at heart, thank you very much," Ashlyn said, patting the empty chair beside her.

"Flattery will get you everywhere," Jane said, slipping in beside her and gazing toward the French doors leading from the parlor. "Uh-oh, I think the big cheeses may have arrived."

Her companions turned in time to spy Kyle Robles standing in the doorway, striking a pose that screamed "Look at me! I'm handsome and important."

Jane rolled her eyes. "Who does he think he is? A dead ringer for Fabio, isn't he?"

Bess elbowed her friend, "Shush!"

"He's gorgeous," Ashlyn whispered. "I hear he's with our hot yoga instructor. Figures."

Robles worked the crowd, stopping at every table to say hello. Of medium height, with a toned body, he had thick, shoulder-length blond hair, which he kept fiddling with. Watching him and his affectation of tossing his head back made Bess dizzy. As he approached their table, his chocolate-brown eyes studied each of them, lingering a bit longer than was polite. "Well, well, well, a table of beauties. Where have you ladies been hiding?"

"We could ask the same thing about you, Mr. Robles," Jane said. "Everyone missed you last night."

"Unavoidable, I'm afraid. And you are?"

"Jane Fellows. My friends Bess and Hillary are from Old Harbor," she added, gesturing toward her companions. "Ashlyn and Jade are from Greenleaf."

"How quaint," he said, obviously already bored and poised to move on. With one more flip of his head, he added, "I look forward to working with you this week. Enjoy your lunch."

Jane rolled her eyes again as they observed Robles greet the guests at the next table, but she refrained from commenting further. Her gaze traveled across the room at a cluster of waitstaff chatting, Angie at the edge of the group, listening. "Our little Angie appears on the outs today."

"She seems a bit of a lost soul, poor thing," Bess said. "Have you three had any conversations with Angie?"

"She seems nice," Hillary said. "Kind of quiet."

"Boring," Ashlyn said.

Jade shook her head. "Ignore my sister. She's a snob and Angie's not her type."

"She's coming this way," Bess said, smiling over the sisters' heads. "Hi, Angie, how are you today?"

"Okay, thanks."

Bess observed her as she took their orders. She looked slightly better than she had at breakfast, her straight hair pulled back in a neat bun, secured with a black scrunchie, blouse tucked in, apron snow white. There was something familiar about Angie, she thought, but then, people often said that about her as well. *We must have common, ordinary faces,* she mused.

"Ms. Demaris? Are you ready to order, or should I come back?"

Startled, Bess realized the young woman had been talking to her. "Oh, so sorry. I'll have the quiche of the day and salad. Thanks, Angie."

"Where were you?" Jane said as Angie headed for the kitchen. "Dreaming of Kyle the magnificent?"

"Very funny. No, just daydreaming."

A half hour later, Jane groaned as she popped the last bite of lunch into her mouth. "That might be the best quiche I've ever had. The pistachio crust was to die for. Think Bella would share the recipe?"

Bess smiled taking a last forkful of field greens, the salad finished with a light, lemony dressing. "It was tasty. Filling was spinach, goat cheese, and maybe some leeks, but you're right. The pistachio crust really made it."

Their companions had all ordered cobb salads, which they pronounced to be "fabulous," in Ashlyn's words. While the other two cleaned their plates, Jade picked at hers and left over half uneaten.

CHAPTER 8

Well prepared and highly organized, Nancy Pratt led a wonderful afternoon workshop on writing and marketing romantic suspense novels. Dressed casually in jeans and a pale blue cashmere sweater, the tiny, energetic author gestured to easels placed around her, holding charts and graphics that augmented her clear, informative PowerPoint slides, the latter of which she provided as a handout.

Bess took copious notes, thankful that Nancy was a member of her critique group. She jotted down a number of questions she hoped to ask at the end of the afternoon or perhaps in their critique group the following morning.

When the workshop ended, Jane and Bess headed up to their rooms. "I think I'll grab my book and relax in one of the porch rockers," Jane said. "You interested?"

"Thanks, but I think I'll close my eyes for fifteen minutes, then do a little writing. I'm surprised to admit, I'm getting excited about writing Helen's next adventure. I even have a plot idea that will be lots of fun to write, if I can pull it off."

"Of course, you can! Happy writing, and I'll knock on your door for the cocktail hour later."

"Perfect." Bess hugged her friend. "Thanks for prodding me into this. It's been so nice to spend time together in this peaceful, lovely place."

"Right back at you," Jane said, blowing her a kiss as she headed to her room.

Bess spent the next hour jotting down her thoughts and a rough outline for the next Anne Greyson book. *Can I pull it off?* she wondered. *It might turn out to be as much fun as reading the books.* She sighed, thinking of Harry Winthrop. What would he think of her bold new venture? He was a generous, kind soul who only wanted the best for those he loved. *He'd love it and be pleased*, she decided, setting her writing journal aside. Tonight, if there was time, she would type up all her scribblings.

Her cell buzzed, and she spied her husband's name. "Hello," she answered brightly. Being away from Roger was the only downside to the retreat so far.

"Hello, my love. How are you doing?"

"Very well. I'm getting some solid ideas for the next Anne Greyson book."

"That's great news. Can't wait to read it."

"I suspect it will be a long, slow process once I get going. How are you doing?"

"Pretty quiet here. I'm heading to Mattapoisett tonight for dinner with Paul Smith. Didn't know when I'd be back and wanted to hear your voice." He referred to the Mattapoisett police chief with whom he was friendly and with whom he had recently collaborated on a case.

They talked awhile, then said their goodbyes. After she clicked off, Bess leaned back against the soft eiderdown pillows and closed her eyes. She had adored her first husband, Macomber, and mourned him for almost a decade. She had also loved, very briefly, the dashing Harry Winthrop, but if she were being completely truthful, Roger was the love of her life, the man she had loved since he'd first gazed at her with those icy-blue eyes that reached in and touched her soul. It had always been Roger. Mac had known it and so had Harry.

∿

Jane's knock startled Bess and she realized she'd dozed off. She hopped up and opened the door. "Can you give me ten minutes? I'd like to take a wake up, shower, and change."

Jane's long red hair was windblown and tangled. She had a satchel over one shoulder and a book in hand. "Me too. Whoever's ready first, come get the other."

The cocktail hour was winding down as the friends strolled in arm in arm. Bess had dressed in a simple peach linen dress with capped sleeves and a slim silhouette, a strand of pearls around her neck. Jane wore an emerald green sheath that hugged her lovely figure in all the right places. They both had chosen well, and heads turned as they made their appearance.

People milled about chatting in small clusters, they ordered white wines from Ron Vickers, who was tending bar. Hillary hurried over to greet them, looking especially pretty in a sleeveless sun dress, a pastel floral print, strappy four-inch espadrilles, and a white shawl over her shoulders. "You two look gorgeous! Where have you been? You missed all the excitement."

"Oh?" Bess said.

"Do tell," Jane echoed.

"Our yoga instructor has quite a temper hidden under her serene façade."

"What happened?" Jane asked. "Don't beat around the bush."

"It appears as if she was pissed at Kyle for being late, but then he lashed out at her. It was quite a scene. Realizing they had an audience, they moved it out to the front porch, but there was a lot of shouting and words like bastard, whore, and cheat flying around. They also seemed to be arguing about her daughter. Finally, Daisy stomped out from the kitchen and told them to shut up. It was ugly."

"Oh dear," Bess said, gazing around. "Where are they now?"

"Kyle and Fawn stomped off in different directions. Daisy's in the kitchen with her buddies."

"Wonder if they'll dare show their faces tonight?" Jane said as their fellow authors began moving toward the dining room.

"They'd better," Claire Rubin said, coming to stand by Bess. "He's giving tonight's workshop."

"Hi, Claire," Bess said, turning to the tall, patrician woman in a red-brick-colored wrap-style cocktail dress with a plunging vee neck. She wore strappy black sandals, silver hoop earrings her only jewelry. It was a bold fashion choice for the usually conservative sixty-something, but it suited her. As Jane and Hillary proceeded into the dining room to locate a table, Bess said, "Haven't had a chance to chat. How are you?"

"Better. I'm not sure if you heard, but Steele and I are separated."

"No, I hadn't. I'm sorry to hear that."

"It was time. I endured life with a serial philanderer as long as I could, but then realized I'm happy and better off on my own."

"I heard that you opened a shop?"

Claire nodded. "Ester McPhee and I took over a very successful children's clothing store, and I'm proud to say we've made it even more successful."

"That's great. Where is it?"

"Marion. That's where I'm living now. Renting a little cottage on the water till I decide where I want to be."

"That's great. Big enough for your grandchildren to visit?"

Claire smiled. "Just barely, but I'm thinking of moving back to Old Harbor within the next year. I loved it at the beach, but I have my eye on a couple of properties. Steele may have been unfaithful, but he's promised to be generous in the divorce and I still have most of what I had with my dear Dickie," she said, referring to her first husband and father of her three grown children.

"That's something at least," Bess said. "Would you like to sit with us?"

"I'd love it, thank you, dear."

The two women made their way to the table Hillary and Jane had secured. No sooner had Claire taken her seat than Yorky Strauss slipped in beside her. "Is this seat taken?"

Claire's cheeks turned red as she smiled at him. "It is now, please."

Bess moved around the table to the empty seat beside Jane. Her friend leaned over and whispered, "Mark my words, there's something's going on with those two. I saw them returning from a very friendly walk earlier."

"Shush," Bess said. "If something's happening, I'm glad for her. He seems like a nice man after you-know-who."

"You know something?"

"Later."

Aside from Claire and Yorky, their group included Hillary, Ashlyn, and Daisy, the latter dragged to the table by Ashlyn. Bella had given Daisy the night off before Kyle Robles's evening workshop. Jade was feeling unwell and elected to have soup in their room.

Most of the meal, Daisy chatted nonstop to anyone who would listen about her poetry, which she proclaimed to be brilliant, and her parents, whom she labeled useless and infantile. Several times, her fellow diners had attempted to change the subject or inject a comment, but mostly they ignored her and enjoyed their delicious dinner of seafood mélange, a beautiful salad of shredded red and green cabbage with a piquant dressing, and crusty artisan bread.

Bess watched Jane, smiling as her friend sopped up every last drop of broth with her bread. "Too bad you didn't like your mélange."

"I'm moving in. This food is incredible. Do you think Bella would share this recipe too?"

"She's writing a cookbook," Daisy said. "The recipe will probably be in there. She even invited my mother, who can barely boil water, to contribute a recipe or two."

"They'll probably be healthy options," Ashlyn said. "I'm always looking for those. Your mom's a fantastic yoga teacher, by the way."

Daisy scowled. "Anyone can teach yoga."

"Not in the sublime way she does," Jane said. "Another reason I must move out here. Is she in residence often?"

"Nope. Just for this week. She comes 'cause Kyle's here."

"Does she teach somewhere near your home?"

"Not my home. She and Kyle live in a loft in Providence, but if I had to guess, they won't be for much longer. Mom teaches at East Side Yoga. The classes are super expensive. Big rip-off."

"Are they moving?" Ashlyn asked.

"Splitting up. Only reason they haven't already is because they both love the loft and no one wants to vacate. It's gonna be a huge fight, but Kyle has the big bucks, so he'll probably win."

"Your dad's books are very popular," Bess said.

"Kyle is not my dad, but yes, he makes millions. Mom makes shit. She's what's called a hanger-on."

Claire and Yorky chatted quietly together, for the most part oblivious to their fellow diners, but suddenly, he sat up and said, "Your mother is far from a hanger-on, my dear. She is a highly sought-after mindfulness expert as well as yoga teacher. As you well know, she has given week- and month-long retreats at Kripalu, Canyon Ranch, and a host of other exclusive retreat venues. I would guess her income comes close or may even surpass Kyle's."

They all stared at him for thirty seconds before Daisy shrugged and mumbled, "Whatever."

"Who has room for dessert?" Angie as asked as she appeared and began clearing their dinner plates.

Daisy pushed back, her chair scraping on the wood floor. "Not me. Excuse me, gang. See you in the morning."

"Aren't you coming to tonight's workshop?" Ashlyn asked.

"No, thanks. Been there, done that. I've heard it all before, believe me. Kyle hasn't anything to teach me. See ya."

As Angie disappeared to retrieve dessert menus, Claire shook her head. "A very unhappy young woman, poor thing. At least she seems confident about her writing."

Jane made a so-so gesture and whispered, "She's in my critique group. Maybe her earlier work is better."

"Or we don't understand some of the new age verse," Bess said.

"Yeah, right. Thanks, Angie," Jane said, taking her menu.

Tonight's special was baked Alaska, which they all decided was a must. Yorky and Claire elected to share theirs along with decaf cappuccinos. The dining room was soon alight with flaming desserts everywhere, oohs and aahs rising from every table.

LATER, FOLLOWING KYLE ROBLES'S WORKSHOP, BESS AND JANE CLIMBED the stairs to their room. "Very disappointing," Bess said. "I mean, the Anne Greyson books aren't thrillers per se, but I was hoping to learn a bit about plotting and creating suspense."

"He's a blowhard. Wouldn't be surprised if he employs a ghost writer."

"Maybe the whole scene with his wife threw him off his rhythm? He must have been embarrassed, don't you think?"

Jane shrugged. "Who knows. I should have done a 'Daisy' and skipped Mr. Boring, Self-Important Robles."

"Can't wait for our morning critique group. I have so many questions for Nancy. I wish she was giving more presentations. I could listen to her for hours."

They paused outside Bess's room. "I'm guessing Beck Bailey's talk will be good," Jane said. "Even if neither of us writes nonfiction. He might help with setting?"

"Want to come in for tea?" Bess asked.

"Thanks, but I'm beat. I'll knock in the morning for yoga."

"Perfect," Bess said, hugging her friend. "Night."

"Sleep tight."

There was a message from Roger on her cell saying he and Pete had been called to a suspicious death in Taunton, so Bess texted him. "Good night. I love you. Be safe, and we'll talk tomorrow."

CHAPTER 9

A scream pierced the silence, and Bess bolted upright, shaking. *Was it a nightmare?* Nightmares were not uncommon since Harry's death. She got up and went to the hall door, unbolting it and peeking out. Silence. Shaking her head, she went to the bathroom, retrieved a glass of water. After taking a few sips, slipped back into bed. The clock on the bedside table read 1:35 a.m. She considered calling Roger. His voice never failed to soothe. Then, deciding not to wake him, she plumped her pillow, rolled over, and drifted back to sleep.

⁓

"Morning!" Pete yelled as he banged open the door of RHD. The Regional Homicide Division was housed in a small cottage, converted a number of years ago into office space. Aside from the ground floor, which was entirely theirs, RHD shared the building with a small Homeland Security office and a satellite office of the FBI, both of which occupied the second and third floors. They rarely saw their fellow tenants. RHD employed several ancillary people, including their forensic team, but Roger, Pete, Greta Burke, and their newest member, Brendan Stevens were its core. Brendan had joined them a year earlier, a short time after his academy graduation, and Greta had been with them for several years.

"You're in early," Demaris said, peering over his glasses as Pete poked his hear around the door. In fact, it was the rare day that either of them beat office manager Lottie Willis into work. Usually, she had bagels spread out and coffee brewing when they arrived. Until recently, it had been donuts until he'd put his foot down and banned sugar from the premises.

"Kind of boring at home without Hill. Anything new come in?"

"No, and after last night's wild-goose chase, I'm hoping to have today to catch up on paperwork. I told Greta to stay put unless we needed her. Brendan too. They both have unfinished reports they can type up from home."

"Me too. Want me to grab coffees down the street?"

Demaris smiled at his second-in-command, who was like a son to him. "Yours is on your desk. Still hot."

Brave, loyal, and protective, Pete had come straight from the academy to Old Harbor Police. Thus, he'd been with Roger since day one. He looked a decade younger than his thirty-six years, and his pale blue eyes and red hair reminded Demaris of a young Ron Howard, aka Opie. Only the angry scar on Pete's forehead pointed to a life beyond Mayberry, a life that had almost killed the young officer. Every waking moment, Roger carried the burden of guilt for that. Never again would he leave a member of his team alone, especially when they were tracking a vicious killer.

"Thanks, boss. Good to have a quiet day, huh?"

"Bite your tongue."

～

"What a morning," Bess exclaimed as she and Jane walked along the path bordered by fields and wildflowers, headed to the yoga studio. It was sunrise, and the eastern sky was aglow with orange and yellow as they made their way in the semidarkness.

Jane nodded. "Gonna be a glorious day."

Bess paused and turned to her. "Jane, did you by any chance hear screams in the night?"

"No, but when I take one of my magic pills, which I did last night, I sleep like the dead. Why?"

"I think it was just a nightmare. Everything was quiet when I got up to check."

"Who knows? Looks like we're the first to arrive this morning. The studio's still dark."

No sooner had she spoken than a light went on in the barn and they heard a bloodcurdling shriek.

"What the hell?" Jane cried as they ran toward the studio.

The door was ajar. They found Fawn Davis crouched over her daughter's lifeless body, sobbing. "Baby, baby, wake up baby. Mommy's here."

When Fawn reached for her daughter as if she meant to cradle her in her arms, Bess cried, "Stop, Fawn, don't touch her. Step back. We need to call the police."

None of them had their cell phone, so Jane grabbed the studio's wall phone and called over to the inn. Fawn stood up, continuing to stare down at her daughter. Daisy's throat appeared to have been cut clean across, her arms and legs splayed out at odd angles. Her pale bare feet poked out from lime-green leggings. Her white top was stained bright red, and a pool of blood ringed the body. Bess stepped closer and put her arm around Fawn's shoulders, surprised to find her completely still.

"Who could have done this?" she asked as if talking to the opposite wall.

After what seemed an eternity, they heard sirens in the distance. Several minutes later, the doors flew open and several officers came in, followed by Paul Smith, the chief of police in Mattapoisett.

"Bess," he said, "I didn't expect to see you here."

"We're on a writers' retreat, Jane and me. You remember my colleague Jane Fellows from Old Harbor Friends?"

"Yes, hello," Smith said, coming forward to shake their hands. Tall and lanky with short sandy hair, Paul had always reminded Bess of

Ichabod Crane. His blue eyes darkened as he turned toward the tiny body crumpled on the floor. "Who is she?"

"My daughter, Daisy," Fawn said, her voice flat.

"And you are?"

"Fawn Davis."

"I'm very sorry for your loss, Ms. Davis." Smith turned to Bess and Jane. "You ladies discovered her?"

"No, Fawn," Jane said. "Fawn was here slightly before us. She found her."

"No one else has been here, then?"

As if on cue, Bella Vickers walked in, followed by Nancy Pratt and Marilyn Lively. "Oh, my goodness, poor Daisy," Bella said.

Smith stepped forward. "I must ask you ladies to step away and go back to the inn. This is a crime scene."

"On my property," Bella said, standing her ground.

"Bella, I'm sure you understand, we can't let any of you in. Our crime scene people will be here soon and the less contamination, the better."

"Now see here, you," Marilyn said, hands on hips. "We're in the middle of a very important retreat."

"And you would be...?"

"Marilyn Lively, author and retreat coordinator along with Nancy Pratt, another well-known author, and my co-coordinator. She waved at Nancy standing beside her, looking vaguely uncomfortable.

"Well, Ms. Lively and Ms. Pratt, I will ask you to accompany Bella back to the inn." Turning to the others, he said, "Bess, Jane, and Ms. Davis, you go too. We'll come find you to take formal statements in a bit."

∼

"Look at this, boss," Pete called as Demaris passed his office door. "They just posted a notice—murder on Gooseberry Island."

Demaris's blood ran cold as he rushed to Pete's side. "What? Does it say who? The victim?"

"Nope, just 'woman murdered.'"

"Get your things. We're going out there now."

"They may have it cordoned off."

Demaris gave him a look. "You're driving. Now, hurry."

Soon after, Pete was racing along back roads to reach the highway, a short time later turning off and driving through the village of Old Harbor and out to the ferry landing for Gooseberry Island. During the drive, Demaris made several calls. When he finally clicked off, he turned to his assistant. "Can't you go any faster?"

"Did they say anything? Couldn't be Hill or Bess, or the other one would've called."

"It's a young woman, Daisy Davis. Paul Smith's men are there, but they're happy to have us join them."

"Thank God," Pete said, letting out a huge sigh of relief. His fingers, white knuckled since they left the station, relaxed on the steering wheel as the Gooseberry Island ferry came into view through the fog ahead.

CHAPTER 10

By the time they reached the inn, the property was enveloped in thick, pea soup fog, the landscape obscured fifteen feet from where they parked. They'd barely stepped onto the lawn when Bess and Hillary rushed down from the porch into their arms.

"You okay?" Roger asked, tears in his eyes as he drank in her familiar scent of citrus and jasmine.

"Now I am," Bess whispered, hugging him tightly.

"So, you two found her?"

"Jane and I came for yoga and found Fawn Davis, the victim's mother, standing over the body. She was just bending down to hug her. It appeared that she had arrived just moments before us."

"Pete and I have got to get out there. You okay with Jane and Hillary?"

"Of course. Go." After one more hug, she let him go.

Pete kissed Hillary. "Be back to check on you later, babe. Ready, boss."

Demaris looked from Bess to Jane and Hillary. "Megan's on her way. Greta too. If you see them, direct them to the studio."

Bess nodded. "Will do."

"Have Bella make you a tea with a healthy shot of brandy."

"This early in the morning? Maybe not," she said. "We're fine. Go."

As Roger headed off, she turned to Jane. "Let's go to breakfast. See what we can find out about people's whereabouts and stuff."

Her friend stared at her. "Stuff? What kind of stuff?"

"Come on." Bess led the way up the porch steps. Jane followed, shaking her head.

The first person they met was Leo, who corralled them in the front parlor. "Ladies! What do you know? I was headed for yoga, but the police turned me away."

Nancy and Marilyn swooped in before either Jane or Bess could reply. "What a tragedy," Nancy said. "Marilyn tells me you two found poor Daisy?"

Jane raised her arms. "Whoa, everyone. Bess and I know nothing. Sadly, her mom found her. We arrived a few minutes later, were sent back here, and, like everyone else, we'll just have to wait to hear what the police have to say."

"They'll be coming over to take everyone's statement soon," Bess added.

"They just called over and spoke to Ron," Bella said, coming from behind the reception desk. "No one's to leave the island."

A small group had gathered now, mostly those dressed for yoga, Wilma Conlon and Claire Rubin among them. Bess looked around for Hillary, who had disappeared, then spied her waving from the dining room door. "Come on! We've got a table," she called, saving them from further interrogation.

Bess and Jane hurried off, Claire and Wilma in their wake. "Might there be room for us?" Claire whispered to Bess.

"Of course," she replied.

They all sat leaving one empty seat next to Claire. Leo approached, clearly wishing to sit with them, but Claire announced that she was saving the place for Yorky. Tallstory gave an elaborate bow saying, "Until later, ladies," and found a seat with Marilyn, her husband, Beck, and Nancy. No sign of Kyle Robles.

"You'd think Daisy's father would have been notified," Jane said.

Bess nodded. "Even though Daisy told us emphatically that he wasn't her father, I can't imagine he wouldn't want to be here to support Fawn. I wonder where she is. Shame if she's alone right now."

Georgia Capuano, one of the waitstaff, appeared to take their beverage orders. Broad shouldered, with a slender waist, Georgia had her dark brown hair tied back in a bun. Her white uniform shirt was already splattered with something orange. "What can I get you, folks? Chef has made cranberry orange waffles as a special this morning."

"Where's Angie?" Jane asked.

"She's around somewhere." As if on cue, Angie swung open the kitchen door, a tray full of cream and sugar dishes in her arms. She set the tray on a sideboard and went to take the orders at Marilyn's table. Georgia circled their table, noting who wanted coffee or tea, then said, "Be back in a sec."

After Georgia served the coffee and tea, she disappeared into the kitchen.

"Hi, Angie!" Bess called as the young woman passed by on her way to the coffee urns.

"Morning, Ms. Demaris. How're you all doing? What a shocker, huh? Poor Daisy."

"Yes, tragic. The staff, her friends, must devastated."

"We are, and scared too. They say no one can leave."

Bess nodded, smiling up at her. "I'm sure it won't be for long. Just until the police do their investigation. If we can support you in any way, let us know."

"Thanks, Ms. Demaris."

"Bess, please."

As Angie turned away and hurried off, they spied Kyle Robles stroll into the dining room. He ignored his fellow diners and went straight to Bella, who was refilling juice pitchers. "I'm gonna take her upstairs," he said. "Could I get something sent up?" The rest of their conversation was muffled by the chatter around them, but Bess assumed he referred to Fawn. *Poor woman.*

CHAPTER 11

"We just got official clearance," Demaris said as he and Paul Smith watched the Mattapoisett officers cordon off the crime scene "But I don't want to step on your toes."

Smith chuckled. "Like that's gonna happen. Rodge, I'm happy to defer to you on this. Makes sense. You have the team and the experience. We can lend support when you need us. Looks like your forensic team's arrived." Smith eyed the door where Megan Kreiger and her assistant Bethany Yuan were coming in laden with bags and equipment.

On their heels were two others, a slender woman of medium height wearing jeans and sweatshirt, flaxen hair in a sloppy ponytail. "Your Greta always looks like she's just rolled out of bed," Smith said.

"Her life is complicated. Her mother's unwell, so she juggles a lot," Roger said, waving at Greta and the young, dark-haired version of Pete who followed behind her. Brendan Stevens always looked put together and sharp, like the mentor he worshipped.

"Looks like the entire RHD's here. Don't need us anymore."

Demaris grinned, patting his friend's shoulder. "We always need you. Thanks, Paul."

He crossed the room and greeted his forensic people. "Morning,

Megan, Bethany. She's all yours. Whatever you can tell us would be helpful. Looks like she's been dead about four or five hours."

Megan tucked her curly brown hair under a surgical cap, then handed one to Bethany. "Sure thing, boss."

"Thanks," he said, then turned to the others. "Greta, Brendan. Thanks for getting here so quickly." Greta Burke and Brendan approached, the latter taking his usual position beside Pete.

"So, we need to find a space. Greta, can you and Brendan head up to the inn and ask Bella or Ron if they have a spot we can use?"

"Will do," Greta said, giving Stevens a nod as they headed off.

Megan crouched over the body, careful to avoid the pool of blood surrounding what remained of Daisy Davis. "Looks like she was grabbed from behind. Throat's slit clean across. Sharp knife. Not much of a struggle, so she may have been drugged. Judging by her body temp, I'd say she died around one or two. We'll know more when we get her on the table. Are we using the county clinic in Northport?"

Demaris turned to his second-in-command. "Pete?"

"I'm waiting on their call."

"Well, call again. We need that lab now," his boss barked.

Surprised at the sharpness of his boss's tone, Pete stepped away to make the call. After a few minutes, he returned. "The lab's ours. They're sending an ambulance now."

"Thanks, buddy. Sorry to snap at you."

"No prob, boss."

Yes, it is a prob, Demaris mused. *Lots of deep breaths.* "Let's head over to the inn. Megan, if you or crime scene finds anything important, call over, okay?"

Krieger nodded, turning her attention back to the tiny figure.

When the two men walked into the inn, they were waylaid by Ron Vickers. "Hey, Roger, long time no see." He held out his hand. The two men had gone to school together through middle school, then Ron went away to boarding school and college. They occasionally ran into each other in the village.

Pete cleared his throat. "It's lieutenant now."

Demaris grinned. "It's still Roger. Good to see you, Ron. Wish it was under better circumstances."

"I'll say. Cute kid. A bit of a temper, but she didn't deserve this. I told your people you can have the other cottage. It's undergoing renovations, but it's reasonably inhabitable. I'll pull the construction crew and send a couple of the kids to clean up. Three bedrooms, if anyone needs to stay, bathroom and semi serviceable kitchen. No stove, but we can get food to you, and I'll have the kids bring a coffee set up, and snacks and drinks to stock the fridge."

"That's great. RHD can reimburse you, so keep track of everything, okay?"

"Not necessary. Gotta get back to the kitchen. Just make a list and I'll have the crew get it over to you after breakfast. I gave your associate the keys."

"Thanks, Ron."

He waved over his shoulder. "Grab coffees to go if you want. There's plenty on the sideboard over there or in the dining room."

"Pete?" Demaris asked.

"I'm good."

"Me too. Let's go over and check in with Greta and Brendan."

They found the two rearranging furniture and pulling chairs and side tables out from the walls where they'd been piled. "Hey, boss," she said. "Bedrooms are great. This is the only room that's kind of a mess including the kitchen. Workable fridge and sink, but not much else."

"This'll do. Thanks, you two. Let's sit down and get organized. We've got a lot of people to interview."

Once they were all seated at a round dining table set up in a bay window alcove, Demaris said, "Okay, let's see where we are."

Fifteen minutes later, the team dispersed, Greta to interview the kitchen staff and Demaris and Pete remaining in the cottage, while Brendan escorted people one at a time back and forth from the inn to be interviewed. Jane and Bess were first. Pete at his side in a

Naugahyde kitchen chair, the two women across from them sitting side by side on a worn, lumpy love seat.

Demaris began. "Where exactly was Fawn Davis when you two stepped into the studio?"

Bess sat up, surprised at his formal tone. "She was standing over the body about to stoop down."

"It looked as if she wanted to hug her," Jane added, "So Bess called out, telling her not to touch the body."

"To your recollection, did she touch her daughter?"

They both shook their heads.

"What about you? Did you touch Daisy?"

"Roger!" Bess said.

Jane glanced from husband to wife, then said, "After telling Fawn not to touch her, we certainly weren't going to. It was obvious she was beyond saving with her neck like that."

"Okay. After the last few days, what were your impressions of the victim?"

"Jane saw more of her than I did as they were in the same critique group."

Jane sat up, grabbing the sofa's arm to keep from falling sideways into Bess. "I hate to speak ill of the dead, but she was a bit of a spoiled brat. Thought she was the greatest poet who ever lived. She was really nasty to her mother. We never saw her with Kyle Robles, her mother's partner, did we, Bess?"

"No, but I got the impression he didn't have much to do with her."

"Oh?" It was all he could do to stop himself from standing and taking his lovely wife into his arms. He hated this process. Clearly, neither Jane nor Bess had anything to do with Daisy Davis's demise.

"Just an impression, that's all."

They chatted for a few minutes longer, then he released them, gazing over at Stevens. "I want to talk to Kyle Robles next. I don't care what he's doing. Bring him here now."

"He's comforting his partner," Bess said.

"Well, he can spare a few minutes. Brendan, see if you can find someone to sit with her while he's gone."

"We'll do it," Bess said. "Jane and I will sit with Fawn."

Demaris paused. Something told him to object, but instead, he shrugged. "Okay, then. Off you go, Brendan, ladies."

CHAPTER 12

Stevens, accompanied by Jane and Bess, knocked at Fawn and Kyle's room, the Oceanview Suite at the far end of the inn's second floor.

Robles opened the door. "Yeah?"

"Lieutenant Demaris requests that you come to the cottage."

"Now? What're you people, crazy? My partner's only child has been murdered and he wants to chat? What the hell. Tell him to cool his jets."

Brendan stood up taller, his hazel eyes steely. "Let me rephrase, sir. I am here to escort you to the cottage for your interview. This is a murder investigation, and time is of the essence."

Bess and Jane stared at the two men, awed by Brendan's change of tone and demeanor.

"Now listen, you," Robles said, glaring at the young officer.

Bess stepped forward, beside Brendan. "Officer Stevens is just doing his job. Jane and I are happy to stay with Fawn until your return."

"And she knows you, does she? Why would I leave her with two strangers?"

"Kyle, that's enough," a voice called from within. "Go, I'll be fine. I certainly don't want to listen to any more of this conversation."

Robles grabbed his jacket from a hook near the door. "Fine." He stepped aside to let Jane and Bess by. "Lead the way, Junior PI."

"It's Officer Stevens," Brendan said.

Jane closed the door behind them. "Good for him," Jane whispered. "He's got spunk, doesn't he?"

Bess nodded, stepping farther into the room. "Fawn? Would you rather have quiet? We can sit in the dining alcove if you like. Just so you have someone with you."

"No, it's fine. Come in and sit."

"Can we get you anything?" Jane asked.

"Actually, I'd love a cup of hot tea. There's a teapot somewhere, even though it reeks of coffee."

"I'll just pop down to the lobby and grab you one," Jane said, turning and heading back out.

Fawn lay on the love seat in the small living room area, one blanket draped over her legs, another around her shoulders. Bess took a chair opposite her on the other side of a glass-topped coffee table, a shadow box full of seashells beneath it. "I'm so sorry for your loss. Daisy was a lovely young woman."

"Daisy was a brat. I could use stronger language, but I'll leave it at that," Fawn said. "She was my daughter and I loved her, but she wasn't easy."

"Do you know anyone who would want to harm her?"

Fawn looked up, her eyes registering surprise. "Not like that. Plenty of people might've wanted to give her a slap from time to time, but kill her?"

Her pale blue eyes were red and her cheeks blotchy, but the normally ethereal yoga instructor otherwise appeared calm, her hands the only part of her in motion as she fingered the edges of the blankets, first rolling, then releasing small sections of the soft wool.

"I take it Daisy didn't live with you and Mr. Robles, then?"

"No. She did until about six months ago, but then moved out to be with her boyfriend, Scott Cameron. Low-life, good-for-nothing if you ask me. He's the reason she quit school. Couldn't bear to be away from him. They live...lived in a crappy little apartment in Bell Haven.

I begged her to come home, but you saw her. No one told my daughter anything."

Jane quietly opened the door. She carried a tray with three ceramic pots, mugs, spoons, cream, sugar, honey, and a small basket of tea bags. She set it on the coffee table and Fawn absently grabbed two Earl Gray bags and plunked them into a pot. Jane and Bess followed suit, selecting Ceylon and green tea respectively. They sat in silence for several minutes then poured their tea into mugs. Bess stirred a spoonful of honey into her tea, the others just cream.

Fawn grasped her steaming mug with both hands, bringing it to her lips. "The warmth feels good. It's so cold."

Jane set her tea down and stood. "Can we turn up the heat?"

"No, ignore me," Fawn said. 'I'm always cold. You know, it occurs to me that Scott's supposed to be arriving today. Someone should let him know. I don't have his number, but it would be on Daisy's phone."

"Maybe the Vickerses have it since he was coming to work for them?" Bess said.

Fawn gave her a puzzled look, then nodded. "That's right. You were there for our spat the other night."

"I could go down and ask Bella or Ron," Jane said.

"Would you? That'd be helpful. Maybe ask one of them to call him if they have the number. Come to think of it, Kyle might have it. Scott was doing a few odd jobs for him, deliveries, pickups. If you strike out with the Vickerses, I can have him phone Scott."

Hand on the door, Jane was startled by a knock. When she opened it, a gangly young man, long, scraggly blond hair in dire need of washing, stood in the hall, fidgeting. "Hey, I'm looking for Fawn Davis," he said.

"And you are?" Jane asked, barring the entrance.

"I'm Scott. I'm Daisy's, her daughter's, boyfriend. I got in just now and they told me to come up to see you. What's the story? Where's Daise?"

Jane looked over her shoulder and met Fawn's eyes. "It's okay," Fawn said. "Come in, Scott."

He crossed the room and stood staring down at her in torn, faded jeans, a Grateful Dead T-shirt and flip-flops. "So, what's going on, Fawn?"

Red eyes looked up at him. "Daisy's dead, Scott. My baby's gone."

His brown eyes widened as he looked around from one to the other of them. "What? How? I just talked to her last night."

"At what time?" Bess asked.

"And you are?"

"Bess Demaris. My friend Jane Fellows and I are...or were attending the writer's retreat."

"Daisy too," Jane added.

"What happened to her? Was it an accident?" he asked to no one in particular.

Bess shook her head. "I'm sorry to have to tell you this, but Daisy was murdered."

Scott reached up, pulling at his hair as if he intended to yank it out by the roots. "This can't be happening. She can't be dead. I just talked to her."

"We've established that," Fawn said. "Now pull yourself together, Scott."

"Pull myself together? I loved Daisy!"

"I did too, but histrionics will not bring her back."

"Where is she? I want to see her."

Bess stood up to face him. "I'm sorry. That's impossible. She's been taken away by ambulance. She'll be with a forensic team for a few days, I expect."

He started pacing back and forth. "Not Daisy, not Daisy," he muttered as the three watched him.

Finally, Fawn said, "You'd better go down and check in with the Vickerses. I understand you're working here for the summer?"

"Hell I am. Not without Daisy."

"I'm sure RHD will want to ask you some questions," Bess said.

"RHD? What the hell is that?"

"It's a regional homicide team that's been brought in," she said.

"Shit," he said, plunking down on the floor cross-legged, head in hands.

"Thanks for coming at this stressful time, Mr. Robles," Demaris said as the man slammed through the door of the cottage, Stevens on his heels.

"Stressful? The word is heartbreaking. I loved my daughter, and her mother's left on her own to grieve so I can come chat with you."

"I understand," Demaris said, eying Pete, who came to sit at their worktable. "I promise to make this as quick as possible. Sit, please. Can we offer you water or juice?"

Robles waved his hand, plopping down in a sagging upholstered chair, Demaris already seated in its twin a short distance away. As he sat, dust puffed up from the chair. "I'm fine. Let's get on with it."

"What can you tell me about Daisy? You called her your daughter. Were you close?"

"Yes, very."

"Did you see her yesterday after your arrival?"

"Yes, we took a walk before dinner, or I should say before she had to report to the kitchen to begin serving dinner."

"Did her mother accompany you?"

He shook his head. "Fawn and Daisy haven't been seeing eye-to-eye lately."

"And why is that?"

"Not relevant."

"Everything is relevant."

"Well, if you must know to satisfy your prurient and obtrusive curiosity, Fawn and I are going through a rough patch. We've discussed separation. It's very upsetting to Daisy. She'd still be living with us if things hadn't gotten so tense with her mother."

"And where was she living?"

"In a shithole apartment in Bell Haven. She and her boyfriend loved it, but them moving out was crazy. We have a huge loft in Providence. Tons of space.”

“Perhaps they wanted their own place? Privacy?”

“They were fine at the loft until the bickering started.”

“So, both Daisy and her boyfriend lived with you?”

“For a few weeks, but it was a disaster. Not only were the women fighting, but Fawn hates Scott. Thinks he’s a bad influence.”

“And what was your opinion?”

“Good kid. A bit skanky, but he’s young. Lots of us were skanky at twenty-one.”

“Does he know about Daisy’s death?”

“Hell if I know. He’s supposed to arrive today to begin work. Should I call him?”

Pete cleared his throat, and Demaris turned to him. “Just got a text from Greta. Cameron’s arrived. That’s the boyfriend’s last name.”

“Has Greta spoken to him?”

“Not yet. He arrived and ran right upstairs to Ms. Davis’s room.”

Robles threw up his arms. “Great, that’s just great. And you left her there with two strangers. I’m done here.”

“No, you aren’t, but why don’t you take a minute and call Ms. Davis.”

Robles pulled his cell out and punched in the number. “Hey, babe, how’re you doing?”

Silence.

“Just heard that Scott’s here.”

More silence.

“You sure? I can come back? Okay, then. I’ll be back soon.”

Robles pocketed his phone, then looked up, glaring at his interrogator. “What else? I’d like to get back to Fawn.”

“Do you know anyone who might wish to harm Daisy?”

He shrugged. “She was a sweetie, but spoiled. I guess she could rub people the wrong way sometimes.”

“But not you?”

“She was a slob. Lazy, never picked up anything, cleaned her dishes, whatever. That did irritate me. I'm kind of OCD and I like things neat, but when I asked her to clean up, she would."

"Where were you last night and in the early hours of the morning?"

Robles shook his head. "You're kidding, right?"

Demaris gazed over at Pete, then back at Robles. "I assure you I'm not. You write thrillers and mysteries, I understand, so you'd understand that that question is asked of everyone in a homicide investigation."

"Honestly, I could write a playbook for you guys, but fine. After my workshop, I took a walk, then went up to the room and read for a while, watched some television, and went to sleep."

"Did you see Daisy?"

"Only at the workshop. She disappeared afterward to hang out with her friends."

"Who were?"

"The staff kids. I don't know 'em well. They all go around in a gang at these places."

"What about Fawn? Was she with you?"

"Where else do you think she'd be?"

"Well, I wondered since you talked about separating."

"We... She has the suite, and I have a single room next door. They're connected by a door."

"And she was in it when you returned from your walk?"

"Where the hell do you think she'd be at eleven at night? Yes. She was already asleep."

"And you know this because?"

"Because I know Fawn. She believes in getting good and consistent sleep."

"So, you didn't actually see Ms. Davis last night?"

"Not once the workshop broke up, but there's no way she's involved in Daisy's death."

"Thank you, Mr. Robles. That'll be all for now."

"I'm heading out of here in a few hours. Fawn knows how to reach me."

"I'm sorry, that's impossible," Demaris said as both men stood up. "We've sealed off the island. No one will be allowed to leave, at least for a day or two."

"Fat chance of that. I'm outta here. I have two prior engagements that I cannot miss."

"You'd better make some calls, then. We can't let you leave. If you'd like one of us to make them for you and explain the situation, we'd be happy to."

"Thanks, but no, thanks," he said, stalking toward the door, Brendan on his heels.

"Brendan," Demaris called as his officer opened the door. "Mr. Robles can find his way back. You stay."

When the door slammed, he turned to Pete. "Call and ask Greta to join us, will you?" He grabbed a water from the fridge and sat at the table, awaiting his team.

"Greta's on her way," Pete said, sitting across from him. "What a prick that Robles guy is. I've read a couple of his books."

"And?"

"Not in the same class as Patterson, Connolly, Clancy, or Follett, but a decent beach read."

"Are Smith's men in position?"

"Yup, at the ferry, bridge, and marina. Unless he swims or a helicopter swoops in to pick him up, he's going nowhere."

"Lucky us," Demaris grumbled as Brendan joined them at the table. He smiled as he noticed that his junior officer was, as usual, dressed exactly like Pete. Stevens idolized Pete and couldn't ask for a better mentor, with the exception of his second-in-command's temper. *Brendan's nature is calm, quiet, and watchful, and that probably won't change, but I've got to find time to talk to hothead about this,* he mused as Greta pushed open the door.

CHAPTER 13

Demaris looked over his glasses at Greta. "So, what's the status at the inn?"

"They were supposed to have critique groups this morning, but they cancelled them. The organizers were going to talk this morning about the appropriateness of continuing with the retreat program in light of the murder. One of them, Ms. Lively, is in favor of continuing. Her words, 'it will give people something to do while they're stuck on this God-forsaken island.' Mr. Bailey, her husband, is scheduled to present after lunch about nonfiction."

"I'd like to speak to the whole group, and the staff, excluding Fawn Davis and Kyle Robles. They're both welcome to attend, of course, but I've just spoken to him, and I'll contact her privately once we decide on an interview strategy. Why don't we order an early lunch, then ask everyone to come to the dining room at one p.m., if they aren't already there having lunch? You three can decide what you'd like to eat—menu's on the counter—then head over, put in the order, and alert the innkeepers and guests about one o'clock. I want to make some calls and check in with Megan."

Pete opened his mouth, then closed it without speaking. He took his role as "right-hand man" seriously and preferred to remain with his boss at all times. Reluctantly, he stood and grabbed a menu, scribbling his choice on a pad of paper and passing it to Stevens.

"Put me down for a BLT on a spinach wrap," Demaris said. "Chips and an iced tea. If you give that to the kitchen, you can pick up the food after you alert everyone about the meeting. And see if you can corral the two organizers, Marilyn Lively and the Pratt woman."

"Sure thing, boss," Greta said, noting down her lunch choice.

When the door closed behind the three, Roger grabbed his phone and called Bess. She answered on the first ring. "Hi."

"Hello, my love. How are you holding up?"

"Fine, Jane and I just left Fawn Davis and thought we might take a short walk before lunch."

"Good idea. The gang is headed over to let everyone know we'd like to meet as a group at one. Have a good walk."

"Is there anything you'd like us to look into?"

"No, stay out of it, please, Bess. At some point, I'd like to hear about your time with Ms. Davis and the boyfriend, but not now. Take good care, and no investigating. There's a killer on this island."

He hung up and called Megan. "Hey, Meg, anything for me?"

"Not much yet. We're running tests. She may have ingested sedatives or another substance, maybe cannabis? Looks like the killer surprised her and it was quick. Severed her aorta, and she bled out in minutes. Unless the person was super careful, they most likely got sprayed with blood."

"Thanks, Megan. Keep me posted. If you can't reach me, call Pete or Greta."

"Will do, boss."

AFTER SAYING GOODBYE TO ROGER, BESS CHANGED INTO SNEAKERS AND knocked on Jane's door. As they descended the stairs to the front parlor, a strikingly handsome man opened the front door and strode toward the unmanned reception desk. Midfifties, with longish sandy-blonde hair and an athletic build, he wore wire-rimmed glasses, khakis, and a blue sport shirt, collar open, no tie. He bobbed his hand up and down on the round metal bell and called, "Hello, hello" to no avail.

Jane stepped forward. They're probably involved in lunch prep. Are you checking in? Were they expecting you?"

He gave them an odd look. "No, and no. I'm looking for Fawn Davis."

"Isn't everyone," Jane said.

"What's that supposed to mean?" he said, giving her a sharp look.

Bess elbowed her friend. "Fawn's probably in her room. She's had quite a shock today. Did she know you were coming?"

"She called me about our daughter, Daisy. I got in the car as soon as I heard. I'm not far away, in Greenleaf."

Mouth agape, Bess stared at him. "You're Daisy's father?"

He nodded. "Do you know Fawn's room number?"

"We can take you there," Jane said, leading him to the stairs. "I'm Jane Fellows, and this is my friend Bess Demaris. We're here for the writers' retreat."

When they reached Fawn's room, Jane knocked. Kyle opened the door.

"She's resting." He gazed from one woman to the other before noticing the third member of their party. "You. I should have known you'd show up."

"She called me." He pushed past Jane and Bess as Fawn called, "Let him in, Kyle."

"Is there anything we can do for you?" Bess asked.

"We're good." Robles stepped back and closed the door in their faces.

The two friends exchanged looks. "Well, that was weird," Jane said. "We never even got his name."

Bess nodded. "I think we should tell Roger about this, but first let's see if we can find Scott. I'm guessing he'll know his name."

"When I was grabbing my sneakers, I saw Scott from my window."

"Oh?"

"He was chatting with a couple of the young staff out on the back lawn."

"Shall we?"

Once downstairs, they spied Clara Vickers at the reception desk and waved. "Hey, ladies, how are you doing?"

"Okay under the circumstances," Bess said. "How are all the young people doing? Were you close to Daisy?"

"We all were in the way you get when you're smushed together day and night doing grunt work. I also knew Daisy from Greenleaf. She was in some of my classes. And Matt, Henry, and Gus were tight with her and Scott. That's how Daisy and Scott heard about the jobs this summer. Scott grew up with Matt and Henry in Northport."

"I'm surprised," Bess said. "We assumed it was because of her parents' involvement with the retreat."

"Are you kidding? Daisy was furious when she found out her mom was teaching yoga this week. Almost quit. I mean she's...she was all right with Kyle being here, but she and her mom couldn't be in the same room without fighting. I can't understand it, 'cause I'm real close to my mom and dad."

Jane stepped forward, lowering her voice. "Speaking of Scott, do you know where he is?"

"In the kitchen. They've already put him to work doing Daisy's jobs. He claims he's not staying, but he volunteered to work to make a little money until the police let people off the island."

"How nice of him," Jane said, not quite successful in keeping the sarcasm from her voice. "Thanks, Clara. See you at lunch."

"Of course. See ya."

As they neared the kitchen doors, one burst open and Angie appeared carrying a large tray of condiments and table settings.

"Hi, Angie," Bess called.

"Hi, Ms. Demaris."

"How are you holding up?"

"Not great, to tell you the truth. I'm totally freaked out by the murder and not sure I want to stick it out for two months."

"The police are sure to find the culprit," Jane said. "The RHD team is top-notch."

"Maybe, but what if some lunatic sneaked onto the island and is waiting to kill someone else? You hear about those things."

Bess observed the young waitress. Angie's eyes were bloodshot, with dark circles under them. She looked as if she hadn't slept in weeks. "Are you okay, Angie?"

"It's my allergies. There's something on this island that's really kicked up my asthma."

"Should you be working? Maybe you should lie down," Bess said, talking the tray from her and setting it on a serving table.

"I'm fine. With Daisy gone, we're short-staffed."

"We heard that her boyfriend, Scott, was taking her place," Bess said.

Angie pushed a strand of hair from her forehead. "That's a laugh. He's completely useless. I mean, not that Daisy was the hardest worker on the planet, especially this week when she was part of your retreat, but he makes her look like employee of the year."

"Do you know where we can find Scott?" Jane asked.

At that moment, they heard a crash and voices from the kitchen.

Angie rolled her eyes. "Scott. Whaddya wanna bet that he's messed something up?"

"Excuse us," Bess said as they headed for the kitchen door. They pushed into the room to find chaos: water, and broken glass everywhere. Clara and Bella were mopping the floor, as Matt and Henry followed them with brooms and dustpans sweeping up the glass. Scott had a wad of soggy towels and was providing what appeared to be ineffectual assistance at the rear.

"Watch your step, ladies," Bella said, gazing up at them. "Can we help you?"

Bess stepped forward. "Sorry to disturb you. We wondered if we might speak to Scott for a minute?"

"Go," Bella said, waving at him. "We'll finish up."

Avoiding the glass and water pools, the three stepped out onto the back porch. As soon as the door closed behind them, he said, "What do you want?"

"First day jitters?" Bess said.

He shrugged, leaning against the porch rail, his white apron already streaked with multicolored stains. "I'm doing them a favor. I'm outta here as soon as they open the ferry."

"I'm surprised they're making you stay," Bess said. "You weren't even here when Daisy was killed."

"That's what I said, but the big cheese insisted."

"The big cheese is her husband," Jane said, regarding him.

Bess stepped forward. "We asked to speak to you because we wondered if you know Daisy's biological father."

"Jerry? Yeah, I know him. He'll probably be swooping in here as soon as he finds out about Daisy."

"Does Jerry have a last name?" Bess asked.

"Cooper. Why? Are the police trying to find him? He's a professor at Greenleaf."

"And he's here," Jane said.

"Figures."

Bess nodded. "We understand that Fawn called him. Were he and Daisy close?"

He shrugged. "Not really. They'd had no contact till about a year ago. She researched on one of those genealogy sites and found him. They get together once in a while."

"Do you have an opinion of Mr. Cooper?"

"Typical old geezer. Thinks he's God's gift to women even though that ship sailed about twenty years ago. He made Daisy happy."

"Was he pleased that she found him?" Bess asked.

"Seemed so. He's kept in touch with Fawn for years, which is another reason that Daisy hated her, for not telling her about Jerry. All during her growing up, Fawn lied and told her she didn't know who her dad was."

"I wonder why?" Jane said.

"Control. Fawn likes to control everything and everyone," he said. "Listen, I've got to get back to work. Is there anything else?"

"One more question—what is Jerry Cooper's subject area or discipline?"

"History. Don't get him started. He's published one book that was nominated for a Pulitzer, and he thinks he's God."

As Scott stalked off, Jane shook her head. "No love lost there, huh?"

"No one seems to like each other around here," Bess said as they strolled around the porch and went in the front door. "My phone's upstairs. I really should call Roger."

"There's his bulldog," Jane said as they spied Pete crossing the parlor.

"Pete, wait," Bess called.

"Hey, Ms. D."

"Never mind that. It's Bess and you know it. Listen, we've just met someone... Daisy Davis's biological father."

"Here? I don't think the boss knows about him."

"That's what we thought. His name is Jerry Cooper."

They filled him in on their interactions with Cooper, then their conversation with Scott Cameron. When they finished, Pete said, "Where is he now?"

"We took him up to Fawn and Kyle's suite about fifteen minutes ago."

"Thanks, ladies. I'll let Rodge know. He may want him at the lunch meeting. See you."

As Pete hurried off, Bess said, "Shoot, we forgot to mention our conversation with Angie. Do you think they'd want to know about that now?"

"We'll catch 'em later, even though I suspect your husband's not going to be happy to hear about our snooping. Come on, no time for a walk. Let's get cleaned up for lunch. We still haven't heard if they're planning to hold the afternoon workshop. I was looking forward to Beck Bailey's talk."

"Probably turn out to be another blowhard," Jane muttered as they climbed the stairs to their rooms.

CHAPTER 14

"So, anything new besides Mr. Cooper?" Demaris asked as the four sat down for a quick lunch. Brendan distributed the sandwiches, and Greta brought drinks from the fridge.

All three recounted their interactions as they had alerted people to the one o'clock gathering. "Kyle Robles caught us while we were knocking on doors," Greta said. "Not a pleasant man. Says he's coming, but Fawn declined. He didn't mention Mr. Cooper."

Brendan had stopped eating and gazed back and forth from Greta to their boss, his eyes wide.

Demaris set down his delicious BLT and gazed at his youngest officer. "Have you got something to add, Brendan?"

"Well, sir... I... well, Mr. Robles was really rude to Detective Burke, sir. He was swearing and, at one point, I was afraid he'd take a swing at us."

"Greta?"

"He's an asshole, boss. If he'd made a move, Brendan and I could have swatted him like a fly."

"Uh-huh, well, we'll set Mr. Robles straight later. Anything else?" They all shook their heads. "Okay, then. I've made some preliminary lists and divided up the interviews. Greta and Brendan, I have you down for Bella and Ron Vickers, the cook, Julee Frey, and most of the writers—Bob Franklin, Wilma Conlon, Nancy Pratt, Yorky Strauss, Marilyn Lively and her husband, Beck Bailey and Hillary's new buddies, Ashlyn Fields, and Jade Temple."

He grinned, looking from Greta to Stevens. "And I want you to reinterview Robles. Let's see how much we can piss him off. I want to know his take on Jerry and Fawn's friendship and also his relationship with Daisy. There's more to that than he's letting on."

"Pete and I will interview Fawn Davis and this Cooper fellow. I'd also like to interview Claire Rubin and Leo Tallstory. Then we'll start on the rest of staff. If one of you can type up the lists and make copies, we can hand them out at the meeting."

Greta crumpled her sandwich wrapper and looked up. "What about Bess and Jane? Won't it look funny if we don't interview them?"

Demaris smiled. "Good thought. Add 'em to your list. They've already been interviewed, but it wouldn't hurt for you and Brendan to have a second chat. They've been snooping around, so make sure they tell you everything about that. There's also a part-time caretaker. Has anyone seen him?"

"George Whipple, Georgie," Brendan said. "He lives in town. He was at home during the time of the murder."

"I'd still like you to speak with him, ask what he's noticed this week."

"Will do, boss," Greta said. "I'll get started typing the lists."

Stevens hopped up. "I can help."

"Thanks, everyone. Pete, if you'd clean up, I want to make some notes before we head over to the inn."

Pete frowned, then rose to complete a task that would have ordinarily fallen to Brendan. Demaris turned to his paperwork, pretty sure what his detective was thinking. *Spoiled brat to my indulgent parent*, he mused, chuckling to himself.

CHAPTER 15

Bess and Jane sat with Claire and Yorky, expecting to see Hillary, Jade, and Ashlyn swoop in. Instead, they were surprised to find Marilyn, Beck, and Nancy Pratt standing over them. "May we join you?" Marilyn asked as she slid into a chair. Flamboyantly dressed, as always, in a bright yellow pantsuit, Marilyn had swept her auburn hair up in a tight chignon. Beside her, the others looked plain and dowdy. In beige linen slacks and a pale pink sweater, Nancy wore her straight, shoulder-length dark hair pulled back with her signature tortoise shell headband. She wore sneakers and bright red lipstick. Beck was in khakis, a blue sports shirt and tie, the latter, no doubt, in deference to his role as afternoon presenter, Bess thought.

"Is there an extra seat for me?" Bob Franklin asked, coming up behind their hosts.

"Of course," Bess said, patting the seat beside her. A minute later, Hillary, Jade, and Ashlyn appeared at the dining room door, and she shrugged. Hillary waved and mouthed, *No problem*, as the trio joined Leo Tallstory and Wilma Conlon.

Angie appeared with a pitcher of water and proceeded to fill glasses and distribute menus. "There are five lunch choices, but Chef will make something special if you don't like these. Can I get anyone something else to drink besides water?"

All except Nancy ordered iced tea, and Angie disappeared. "She looks a little perkier now," Jane whispered.

Bess nodded as she quietly observed the interplay between Yorky and Claire. Clearly smitten with each other, they appeared to be in their own world, ignoring their fellow diners.

"A budding romance for sure," Jane whispered, following her friend's gaze, then smiling at Marilyn, who clearly disapproved of her secret communications.

Bess took a sip of water before turning to Bob Franklin on her other side. "How's your novel progressing?"

"Slowly, very slowly," he said, chuckling. "Might be time to throw it overboard. I miss Margie. She was such a great reader. She could have given me some pointers."

Bess patted his hand. "We all miss Margie."

He nodded. "Thank you." In his fifties, Bob was bald and round, his cheeks rosy and red from a life spent outdoors. His sea-blue eyes filled with tears. "She was a sweet gal, my Margie. Much warmer and more loving than Glynnis, but don't tell Rosemary I said that about her mother." Bob's second wife, Margie, had been murdered a few months earlier, and his first wife, Glynnis, mother of his only child, Rosemary, had died in her thirties of breast cancer.

Before Bess could reply, Angie appeared with a tray of their drinks and distributed the teas. "Everyone ready to order?" she said in a cheery, almost giddy voice.

Since Fawn had requested lunch in her room, Roger and Pete waited in the parlor for twenty minutes after her lunch had been delivered, then headed upstairs. They met Kyle Robles in the hallway. "You're not gonna bother her now, are you? She's eating lunch."

Demaris nodded. "We can wait. Is Mr. Cooper with her?"

"Unfortunately, yes."

He brushed by them and headed for the stairs.

"Prick," Pete muttered under his breath.

"Come on, bulldog," his boss said as he knocked on Fawn's door.

Jerry Cooper opened the door. *Another preppy academic*, Demaris thought.

Very tall, with longish sandy-blonde hair, an athletic build, and wearing wire-rimmed glasses, khakis, and a green sport shirt, collar open, no tie, Cooper stared down at them. "Can I help you?" His tone was slightly less rude than Robles's.

Badge out, Demaris stood ramrod straight, facing the much taller man. "Lieutenant Demaris, and this is Detective Dugan. We're investigating Daisy Davis's death. We're here to speak with Ms. Davis."

"She's resting."

"No, I'm not!" Fawn called from within.

"Mr. Cooper, I'm guessing? We'll need to speak with you later, so please do not leave the island."

"What could I possibly have to add that's relevant? I wasn't here when someone...someone brutally murdered my daughter."

"We'll decide what's relevant, Mr. Cooper. Now we'll have to ask you to step out while we speak to Fawn."

Arms crossed, Cooper barred the door. "Like that's happening."

"Pete."

Before he knew what was happening, Dugan lifted him up and deposited him in the hallway.

"I believe they're still serving lunch. Perhaps they'll fix you something," Demaris said. Pete closed the door behind them.

They found Fawn stretched out on a love seat, the remains of lunch in front of her—half-eaten sandwich, half a cup of soup, and a salad, which looked untouched, the dressing on the side unopened.

"Fawn," he said, taking her hands in his own. "I'm so sorry for your loss."

"Oh, Roger," she said, standing and throwing her arms around his shoulders. "How could this have happened to my baby?"

Pete watched dumbfounded as the two stood locked in their embrace. Finally, she settled back on the sofa like the Queen of Sheba, and his boss pushed a small coffee table aside, then pulled up a straight backed chair to face her. Pete sat to the left of the love seat.

In yoga pants and a long flowing sage-colored sweater that brought out the green in her aquamarine eyes, she smiled a beautiful smile and flipped her long blonde hair behind her. "It's been a while," she said. "Have you kept up the yoga and meditation?"

He nodded. "Most days. They're kind of essential to me now."

She gave him a wan smile. "Good. They can be life-changing."

"Yes."

"But of course, this isn't a social call. You're here about my Daisy, another life-changing moment."

"Yes."

"Have you made any progress finding out who would...the identity of the monster who killed my baby?"

"Just starting our investigation. Interviews all afternoon and evening. We'll get him or her, I promise. We won't keep you long, but are you up to answering a few questions?"

She waved her hand. "Of course. Please, ask away."

"Can you think of anyone who might want to harm Daisy?"

Fawn shook her head. "No, no one. Everyone loved her. I mean, she could be difficult at times, but her friends loved her."

"Tell me about her friends."

"Honestly, I'm not sure. I meant her childhood friends. I'm embarrassed to say I'm not sure who she's been spending time with lately. I'm sure you've heard, we haven't been on the best of terms this past year. Daisy's been living in Bell Haven with the boyfriend. He apparently has a large circle of friends, including several of the staff here at the inn."

"And they would be?"

"A couple of the busboys, Matt and Henry. Not sure of their last names. Then there's Angie. She lives in Northport, I think."

"All part of Scott's gang?"

"Maybe. I'm not sure. Since Daisy's been here, she seemed chummy with Clara, Ron and Bella's daughter, and Georgia, another of the maids. Georgia's ex-boyfriend, Gus, another staff member, dropped out of Greenleaf last year, and now works here all year round. Daisy's been hanging around with Gus and Georgia, who'll be a junior at Greenleaf next fall."

"No problems with any of them that you know of?"

She shrugged. "Not that I observed. Only person she seemed to have a problem with was me."

"What happened?"

"I made one too many comments about her boyfriend, who I think has dragged her down. Daisy needs...needed to be in school, not hanging around Bell Haven picking up crap jobs when she could get them."

"I understand she was close to Mr. Robles?"

"Kyle had the easy part. Mr. Cool to my trying to enforce a few rules and some structure. He's never had a kid. Doesn't know or appreciate the role of a parent."

"What about Mr. Cooper, the biological father? Was he close to Daisy?"

"No and yes. She just recently learned of his existence. Another reason for her anger at me. She was furious that I never told her about him."

"I understand that you two kept in touch?"

"Crazy as it sounds, part of my heart still belongs to Jerry."

"Was there a reason you two didn't stay together?"

Fawn arched her eyebrow. "Is this necessary for your investigation?"

"Maybe... It's hard to know what's relevant, and answers sometimes lie in one's past."

She rearranged herself on the love seat, pulling a blanket over her legs before meeting his dark blue eyes. "Fine. Jerry is Jerry. Not exactly stable, never faithful. We met at a weeklong wellness retreat. I was twenty-eight at the time, Jerry nine years older. I was what you'd call a free spirit, a bit of a slut, actually. Jerry and I were just participants. We met the first night. The retreat was a joke, a weeklong hookup party with some daily workshops to break up the orgies going on outside of class. I wasn't into yoga then, just men. I swear we all went for the sex and didn't give a shit about wellness. Who does at that age?

"Jerry was the biggest lech of all. Slept with a half dozen women that week. I wasn't the only one he got pregnant. His future wife, Sally, walked away with child as well."

"Oh?"

"Yeah, they married, had two kids, and then divorced, or at least separated. I'm not sure. She was his second wife. As I said, he was a lech. Still is from what I understand, although his boyish charm may be slightly faded."

"Where do his estranged wife and other offspring live, do you know?"

"I think Sally still lives in Greenleaf and maybe the kids too? Daisy got in touch with her half sister, Ruth. They met a couple of times this past year."

"How did that go?"

Fawn shrugged. "I haven't the faintest idea. She refused to tell me anything about her time with Jerry or Ruth. Payback for keeping her father a secret. According to Jerry, Ruth and Daisy became best friends, but you can't really believe anything he says."

"Anything else you think we should know?"

"No," she said, sighing deeply. "Thank you for excusing me from the post-lunch gathering. I'm not sure I could take all the feigned looks of sympathy."

"Why feigned?" Roger asked.

"Daisy's been a little bitch to more than a few people this past week. Her foul mood and anger at finding me here spilled over to a few people, I fear."

"Anyone in particular?"

"I heard from Bella that she was snapping at her staff buddies and had also been a bit boastful and haughty in her critique group."

"Who was in that group?"

"Your wife's friend Jane and that mousy little librarian."

"Wilma?"

She nodded. "Nancy Pratt joined them briefly. Even though she writes novels, romantic suspense, I think, the workshop leaders were trying to check in with each group."

"Well, thanks, Fawn. We'll let you rest. If you think of anything else that might prove helpful, please call one of us. My cell and the numbers of my team are all on here," he said, handing her a card.

He and Pete excused themselves and closed the door to a silent hallway. "Thoughts?" Demaris asked, turning to his detective.

"Some people's lives are messy, huh, boss?"

Demaris chuckled. "Something like that. Come on. Let's make our lives even messier."

CHAPTER 16

"So," Jane said, as she turned to Marilyn Lively. "Have you and Nancy decided whether to go on with the retreat activities?"

Marilyn's violet eyes studied her. She batted her thick, double-layered eyelashes before answering. "Nance and I made the decision to continue the retreat for now, until we're all released. We have today planned, and she and I will give tomorrow morning's workshop on writing series. We'll meet in critique groups in the afternoon, then see where things stand. Honestly, it seems rather macabre to continue, but what else are we to do? We're stuck here."

"Probably for the best," Bob said. "Keep everyone occupied."

"Did you know Daisy well?" Bess asked, directing her question to Marilyn.

"Only through her mother. I've known Fawn for years. Daisy used to be a lovely little girl."

"You and Fawn are longtime friends, then?"

Marilyn frowned for a second, then forced a smile. "Yes, and I've attended her yoga classes for years. She's an amazing teacher."

"Yes, she is," Bess said, turning to spy Angie setting down a large tray holding their lunches.

As plates were distributed, Jane leaned over and whispered, "Didn't your hubby say no investigating? Hmm?"

"Shush," Bess said, looking up. "Thanks, Angie. This looks great."

"You're welcome." Angie gazed around at the table. "Can I bring anyone anything else?"

"Ketchup," Bob said, "and vinegar, if you have a bottle handy?"

"Of course," Angie said, smiling at him. "I'll bring water and tea over in case anyone wants refills."

As Angie disappeared, Claire said, "She's a sweet, kind soul, isn't she?"

"Poor thing. Seems like the other staff exclude her sometimes," Yorky said.

Marilyn waved her hand. "Young people. Inscrutable. Who knows who they deem cool from one minute to the next."

"How did she land here for the summer?" Claire asked.

"Apparently, she's friends with Georgia Capuano, one of the other waitstaff," Jane said. "They both go to Greenleaf, as does Gus, Georgia's boyfriend."

"Does anyone here know someone at Greenleaf?" Bess asked.

Another frown from Marilyn. "If you mean Jerry Cooper, yes. He's a friend of Fawn's, but I can't imagine why he suddenly popped up. And how did he get on the island?"

Bess shrugged. "I don't think they'd keeping people out, just those of us here during the murder have to stay in."

Marilyn waved her hand in disgust. "So, he's allowed to waltz off and on the island as he pleases while we're prisoners? This murder business is getting tiresome. How are Nancy and I supposed to plan? So much work went into this week."

Nancy gave her codirector a horrified look. "It's only been a day, and poor Daisy."

"Mar, have a little heart," Beck said, patting his wife's shoulder.

She wriggled away from his touch and scowled at her coleader. "Don't be tiresome, you two."

Angie returned with Bob's ketchup and vinegar under one arm and two pitchers of water and tea. Deftly sliding the condiments down beside Bob, she began circling the table.

Claire gazed up as Angie filled her iced tea glass. "What are you majoring in at college, Angie?"

"Sociology with a minor in history. I only have one semester left. I should have graduated last year, but I took some time off. A lot of kids do."

Claire nodded. "That's always wise. My son, Dickie, took a year off. Best decision for him. He came back with a much clearer sense of where he wanted to go."

As Angie moved around the table, Jane looked up at her. "If you're a history minor, you must know Professor Cooper?"

"Everyone knows him. He's famous. Almost won the Pulitzer for his *United We Stand* book about protesting and standing up for ourselves. He's kind of like a god at Greenleaf."

Jane exchanged looks with Bess. "Have you ever taken a course from him?"

"Only my freshman seminar. His upper level courses get filled up really fast by majors. If you'll excuse me?"

Without waiting for a reply, Angie hurried off and disappeared into the kitchen. As they enjoyed another delicious meal, the conversation turned to writing. Just after the remnants of lunch were cleared, Demaris and his team appeared at the parlor doors.

THE ROOM QUIETED, AND ALL EYES TURNED TO DEMARIS. HE STEPPED forward, and the others fanned out, standing at various spots along the walls of the room. The entire inn staff had arranged themselves along the far wall near the kitchen as well. The only persons not present were Fawn Davis and the caretaker, George Whipple.

"Thank you, folks. I'm Lieutenant Demaris from the Regional Homicide Division. RHD was called in to investigate the death of Ms. Davis. With me are Detectives Dugan and Burke, and Officer Stevens." As he said their names, each put up a hand.

"Throughout this afternoon and evening, we will be asking each of you to step out for a short interview. I promise we'll be as brief and unobtrusive as possible, but it's imperative that we speak to everyone." As he spoke, Pete, Greta, and Brendan passed around schedules. "You'll see we've assigned each of you a time to talk with either Detective Dugan and myself or Detective Burke and Stevens. The times are approximate. We'll assume you'll be here attending a workshop, in your room, or in the inn's public spaces. Please make yourself available during your allotted time and one of us will come to collect you. Are there any questions?"

He spied a hand raised at the back of the room. "Yes, Mr. Robles?"

"I notice that your wife and Ms. Fellows' names are not included here."

"Already interviewed."

"As was I."

Demaris took a deep breath. "You're quite right. Everyone, if you could mark your schedules to include Bess Demaris at six and Jane Fellows at six thirty. We left the dinner hour time slot open for just this reason. Thank you. Any other questions?"

Wilma Conlon raised her hand. "Do you have any idea when we'll be released? I have cats at home that need me."

"So, you hadn't made arrangements for them knowing this was a weeklong retreat?"

"I only live twenty minutes away. I'd planned to pop home each day between sessions."

"And you no longer wish to stay should the retreat go on?"

"I'm not sure, but either way, I could go home, you see."

"Of course."

"Inspector, do all of us have to listen to this?" Marilyn called, not even bothering to raise her hand.

"All set," he replied. "Unless anyone else has a question?" When the room fell silent, he nodded. "All right, then. Would Ms. Rubin come with Detective Dugan and me, and Mr. Franklin with Detective Burke and Officer Stevens? Thank you for your patience and cooperation." With a quick glance at Bess, he turned and stepped out of the room. Pete moved forward, standing next to Claire, waiting to escort her to the cottage.

As Greta and Brendan approached their table, Bob Franklin stood. "Figures, the one workshop I was really looking forward to and I'm going to miss the beginning."

Bess smiled at him. "We'll take good notes and share them at dinner."

"Thanks," he said, then followed Greta and Brendan, who were conducting their interviews in the Vickerses' private study at the rear of the building.

As Demaris crossed the front parlor, Pete and Claire behind him, Jerry Cooper caught up with him. "Inspector, wait!"

He turned to face the man. "It's lieutenant. We don't usually have inspectors on this side of the pond. What can I do for you, Mr. Cooper"?

"It's Dr. Cooper, but you can call me Jerry. I just wanted to know if I'm free to go?"

"After your interview, I don't see why not."

"Well...what I mean is, I could stay, if it would be helpful?"

"I think we'll be all set."

"No, I mean for Fawn. If nothing else, it'd piss Robles off. He hates me."

Not wanting to continue the conversation within Claire's earshot, Demaris said, "Perhaps when we speak, you can tell us why Mr. Robles dislikes you. Now, if you'll excuse us." Not waiting for a response, he turned and walked out the door.

CHAPTER 17

"Who was that odious man?" Claire asked, as they walked the short distance to the cabin.

"Jerry Cooper, a professor at Greenleaf."

"Really? Why is he here?"

"Fawn called him. Apparently, they're close."

"I was watching him during lunch. He was very rude and abrupt to the staff."

"Hopefully, he'll take the opportunity to go home after his interview."

Once they'd settled into their seats at the cottage and Claire had declined the offer of something to drink, Demaris began. "How are you, Claire?"

"Up and down. It's been a tough year. You might have heard that Steele and I split up?"

"Yes, I'm sorry." Although he really wasn't. Steele Rubin was a cruel, nasty philanderer who had made his wife's life miserable.

"I'm not. We never should have married. After I lost my dear Dickie, I thought Steele might be a strong, comforting partner, but he proved to be just the opposite."

"Dickie was a good man," he said, thinking back on her first husband who had died in a car accident nine years earlier. Claire and her partner, Ester McPhee, owned a successful children's clothing store in Mattapoisett. Her bearing and patrician good looks, not to mention her connections, had attracted the wealthy, snobbish Steele Rubin, but she soon found that he wasn't what he seemed.

"Yes, he was," she said, nodding.

"How were you enjoying the workshop? Before the murder I mean?"

"Very much. Lovely people, or at least some lovely people. Bess may have told you that I've been spending quite of bit of time with one of my fellow writers, Yorky Strauss. Agreeable man, very kind and respectful. After Steele, it does worlds for one's confidence to discover that there are still good men in the world."

He smiled. "Steele Rubin didn't deserve you, Claire. Don't let his cruelty undermine your strength and confidence."

"Thank you. Now, how can I help? I'm sure my love life isn't what you wanted to speak with me about."

"No. And I've barely spoken to Bess, so I hadn't heard of your new friendship with Mr. Strauss. I'm happy for you."

"Thank you."

"Is Mr. Strauss local?"

"Now he is. He's a retired physician. He had a family practice in Barrington for many years. He's recently divorced. When they split up, his wife kept their home in Barrington and he moved to Southport, to a small beach house where they'd spent summers. I haven't seen it, of course, but it sounds lovely. Right on the water."

"Did either you or Dr. Strauss know Fawn and Daisy Davis before the retreat?"

"I'd never met Daisy, but I took a yoga class from Fawn a while back while visiting a friend in Providence. She's a gifted teacher."

"Yes, she is."

Claire looked at him in surprise. "Have you taken her classes?"

He nodded. "I spent some time at Kripalu a few years ago. She was teaching there then."

"Oh, I love Kripalu!" she said, referring to the popular yoga center in western Massachusetts.

"What about Dr. Strauss? Did he know the Davises, do you know?"

"He only knew of her, I believe. His ex-wife took her classes."

Fawn does get around, doesn't she? he mused before asking, "Tell me about last night."

"Well, after supper and the evening critique groups, Yorky and I shared a nightcap on the porch. As we were crossing the parlor, we saw Daisy stalk off in one direction and Fawn in another and it appeared as if they'd been quarreling."

"Oh, in what way?"

"Both were scowling, and Fawn had tears in her eyes. After her very public spat with Kyle and Daisy, it was obvious to all that mother and daughter were not getting along."

"Anyone else around?"

"Just Bess and Jane headed out for a walk. They were coming downstairs as we stepped out the front door."

"Did you hear anything out of the ordinary during the night?"

"I didn't, but I always take a sleep aid when I'm away from home. Knocks me right out. Yorky did mention hearing a woman screaming, but it was only for a second, and he thought he may have been dreaming, so he went back to sleep. Poor Daisy. Maybe he could have saved her if he'd gotten up and called someone."

"I'm afraid by the time he'd have sounded the alarm, Ms. Davis would have been gone."

"Her death was quick, then? That's a mercy at least," she said, more to herself than him.

"Well, thank you Claire," he said, standing. "We'll let you get back to the workshop. Pete will walk you back."

"Of course." She stood on shaky legs. "I have to tell you, after the deaths in the village a few months ago, this is very unsettling. How could such a little place have so much misery?"

"Take care," he said, as he watched her disappear. *At least she'll have Dr. Strauss by her side to weather this one and not that pompous ass of an ex-husband.*

⁓

B ECK B AILEY'S WORKSHOP PROVED TO BE MUCH MORE INTERESTING THAN Bess had anticipated. His remarks about the integral role of setting had her taking copious notes. Bailey's demeanor seemed totally transformed as he spoke, his presence and commanding voice so different from when he was acting as Marilyn's sidekick.

"There goes our resident buffoon," Jane whispered as Pete quietly escorted Leo Tallstory out for his interview.

"Hush," Bess said, elbowing her while stifling a chuckle. As Tallstory squared his shoulders and strode from the room, she smiled, thinking of her husband interrogating him.

As the question period began, she turned her attention back to their speaker.

⁓

"M R. T ALLSTORY, THANK YOU FOR JOINING US," D EMARIS SAID, GAZING up at the tall, gangly man who stood almost a foot taller than his five-five.

"Very inconvenient, as I had several questions for our speaker."

"I'm sure you can ask one of the others to fill you in, and there's always the dinner hour."

"Yes...well," he said, swishing down on the love seat, then staring at his interrogator with watery hazel eyes. He appeared to have stepped from the pages of a Victorian romance novel in vest, morning coat, tapered charcoal-striped pants, and shiny black boots. "Let's get this over with."

Taken aback by the man's appearance, Demaris almost asked where he gotten his extraordinary attire, but instead took a breath and began, first with the man's whereabouts the evening before.

"In bed, sound asleep, heard nothing."

There was something very rote and rehearsed about his story, like he'd told it many times and was bored. When asked about his fellow workshop attendees, he waved his hand. "Strictly amateurs, except for Kyle, Marilyn, and Nancy."

"That surprises me," Demaris said. "I understand that Beck Bailey's books are well respected and the young women who write the pet mysteries do pretty well, according to my sources. I also think Bella Vickers sells well."

"Exactly!" Tallstory said, waving to Pete. "Could I possibly have some water?"

Pete opened his mouth, then shut it, standing to fetch a bottle from the fridge.

"What do you mean by exactly?" Demaris asked as Pete handed the bottle to Tallstory.

"Cooking capers? Pet mysteries? I mean, really, who takes those seriously?"

"Genre fiction, aren't they? Similar to what the rest of you write, with the exception of Mr. Bailey." He knew he was way off track, but couldn't resist baiting the man. Before Tallstory could reply, he said, "I understand you teach part-time at Greenleaf? What's your subject?"

"English literature."

"Not writing."

"Hardly."

"So, you must know Jerry Cooper, Daisy's biological dad?"

"Our paths have crossed a few times, but I wouldn't say I know him. Impresses me as kind of a dilettante."

Pot calling the kettle black, Demaris thought. "What about the kids?"

"Excuse me?"

"Several of the summer staff go to Greenleaf. Did you know them from school?"

"First of all, I'm an adjunct at Greenleaf, so I teach my classes, hold office hours, then leave. I certainly don't fraternize in the student union."

"Do you recognize faces when you're dining or roaming about the inn?"

"I don't roam. I make it a rule to focus on the event. Period. Wait-staff, household staff, whoever, are invisible to me."

They talked a few minutes more. When Tallstory rose to leave, he paused and turned to Demaris. "There was one odd thing. As I turned in last night, I gazed out my window at the ocean and saw two people walking along the cliffs. One was blonde. It could have been poor Daisy. Hard to tell in the darkness. I remember thinking it was an odd time to be out for a stroll, but then assumed it was some of the young people. I remember hoping they'd go to bed soon to forestall my breakfast getting dropped in my lap by hungover waiters."

"What did the other person look like?"

He shrugged. "About Daisy's height. They were wearing a hooded jacket. He or she turned and looked right up at me, but his or her face was shrouded in darkness. Then I pulled the curtains and went to bed."

"Well, thank you," Demaris said. "If you think of anything else, especially recollections related to the pair on the cliffs, please let us know. All our cell numbers are on the card Detective Dugan is passing to you. Please call day or night."

As Pete and Tallstory disappeared, he made a note to query anyone with an ocean-view room about the mysterious pair, one of whom might have been Daisy.

CHAPTER 18

Beck Bailey fielded the last of his audience's questions, then Nancy stood and thanked him and everyone for "a lively exchange of ideas." As the group dispersed, Bess spied Matt Crowley, one of the waitstaff, chatting with a couple of his buddies. Of medium height, with brown eyes, dark curly, longish Heathcliff hair, he was a handsome young man, and he knew it. Sporting a T-shirt with a voluptuous blonde depicted below the message "Party till she's cute," he leaned back again the windowsill, grinning.

"Let's go chat with Matt," she whispered to Jane, who looked at her in surprise before shrugging and falling in by her side.

"You're going to be in big trouble if you-know-who finds out," Jane said as they neared the group.

"Hi, guys," Bess said, adopting a cheery "I'm cool" tone. It had no effect, and the three young men stared at her as if she were an alien. "Matt, right? Have you got a minute to talk with my friend Jane and me?"

"About what?"

His scowl was not reassuring, but Bess plunged ahead. "We just wondered how all the staff is doing after Daisy's death."

His companions drifted off, no doubt wanting to avoid being

interrogated next. Matt looked ready to follow them, but Jane stepped to the side, blocking his escape. "Nice T-shirt."

He shrugged, giving her an insouciant grin that probably worked well on younger women, but irritated Bess. "Where were you last night? Did you hear or see anything odd?"

"I told your husband everything I know, which is squat, so why don't you ask him?"

"Humor us," Jane said, hands on hips, giving him the evil eye. "Did you know Daisy very well?"

"I knew her through Scott, that's it. Didn't see anything last night. A couple of us were drinking beers down on the beach."

Bess asked, "Who was with you?"

"Not that it's any of your business, but Henry and Gus. We invited Georgia, but she crapped out. Said she had stuff to do."

"Not Angie?"

"We told her about it, but she said she was hanging with Clara."

"So, Clara and Angie are friends?"

"What do I know? They hang out sometimes 'cause neither of them drinks and the rest of us like to party on our off hours. Listen, I gotta go. This is the only break we get all day. By the way, Henry and Gus'll tell you the same story. Angie and Georgia too."

"Sorry to hold you up."

"No prob. See ya."

As Matt disappeared through the kitchen door, Pete came up behind them. "Hey, Bess, Jane. You ladies aren't questioning people, are you?"

"No, just chatting about what's for dinner."

He raised an eyebrow, gazing from one to the other. "Better not be, or there'll be hell to pay from the boss."

"No worries!" Jane said, taking hold of Bess's hand.

"Are you finished interviewing for the day, then?" Bess asked.

"Nope. Coming for the Capuano kid. Have you seen her?"

"I think she's in the kitchen," Jane said.

As he gave them one last look, Pete said, "And don't forget. It'll be your turn soon."

Jane saluted him. "Aye-aye, Detective. Do we have time for a walk?"

"Yup, we've got Georgia Capuano, then Jerry Cooper and one of the other busboys before you."

As they waved goodbye, Jane said, "All right, Ms. Marple. We have a couple of hours before dinner, and I desperately need a walk."

After changing into sneakers, the pair headed off along the cliff path circling the island. A sunny afternoon, the ocean's deep blue below them, they walked at a brisk pace, chatting about the murder, writing, school, and life. The two women had been through so much over the years, from the death of Mac, Bess's first husband a decade earlier, Jane's affair and breakup with the school's former headmaster, and the murder of Bess's fiancé, Harry Winthrop, the previous year. While Jane was still single, she had made a connection with one of Harry's friends, Tim Hargreaves. No dating yet, because Jane claimed she wasn't ready, but he had promised to stay in touch. Finally, there was Bess, who had found love again with Roger, her high school sweetheart.

A half mile from the inn, they heard rustling in the bushes growing along the cliff. "Some kind of animal, do you think?" Jane asked.

"Sounded more like someone threw something in there like a rock?" Bess said as the two moved closer to an opening in the brush.

"There's a path here," Bess said. "It's overgrown, but it could lead to the beach. It looks slippery, though."

As Jane came up beside her, peering down into the darkness of the brush-covered path, they heard movement behind them. Before either could turn, they were shoved hard, propelling them downward along what was, indeed, a slippery steep incline. Jane screamed as they tumbled and rolled, clutching on to one another in the darkness. After what seemed like hours, but was probably only a few seconds, they found themselves hurtling through the air. They landed with a thud on soft sand.

"Ouch," Bess cried as she tried to sit up.

"Are you okay?" Jane asked, brushing off the sand. "Where are we?" She looked around, then helped Bess to her feet. They stood in a cave with smooth rock walls. The path had ended ten feet above them, and they'd been propelled off a ledge of rock that circled the cave's roof.

"I don't know, but my shoulder's bruised. I hope I didn't dislocate it," Bess replied, holding her left arm against her side.

"Oh, gee." Jane pulled off her sweater and wrapped it around her friend's shoulder. "Let me look around, then I can help with that. My sister was always dislocating her trick shoulder."

Bess looked at her, eyes wide. "What are we going to do? There's no way out of here."

Jane hugged her. "Start yelling. Someone's got to hear us."

As she spoke, the ocean crashed outside their prison, water seeping in through openings in the boulders too small for them, but not rising waters.

"Do you think this space gets flooded at high tide?" Bess asked.

"Let's hope not," her friend replied, gazing around, searching for an escape route. "Okay, let's get your shoulder back in place and plan our next steps. Don't be afraid to scream out in pain. Any noise we can make is great."

CHAPTER 19

Georgia Capuano had little to add to their queries. She'd spent the evening in her room, chatted with her boyfriend from home, didn't go out or see anyone on the cliff path, and had no idea where the rest of her fellow staff spent the evening. She confirmed that Matt had invited her to join them on the beach and that she had declined. She knew most of the staff from Greenleaf, but said they weren't close. "I mean, I grew up with those doofuses. Do you think I'd rush to hang out with them in college? No way."

As the interview concluded, Demaris thanked her, and she stood. "Gotta get back and change before dinner prep. Thank God they give us four sets of pants and shirts. These are gross by the end of the day." She waved at her shirt, which was dotted with red spots that appeared to be ketchup or tomato sauce, its crisp white a faded memory.

Not what one would call pretty, Georgia was nonetheless striking. She carried herself with confidence and her posture was perfect. As he watched her depart, Demaris imagined she ruled the roost in the kitchen and dining room. As she opened the door, he called, "Georgia?"

She turned, brown eyes gazing at him. "Huh?"

"I understand all the staff rooms are on the third floor?"

She nodded. "Lucky us, up with the cobwebs and crap."

"Does someone share your room?"

"Julee and Maeve," she replied, referring to the cook and housekeeper. "I lucked out. They're year-rounders. They move in together during the summer, but live in town the rest of the year. When we all came out for orientation, Bella asked them who they'd be willing to share the room with, and they said me."

"And the others?"

"The guys are all together in a bunk room, and Angie has a crappy little single that only fits a bed and a tiny table. No bigger than a closet. In fact, I think that's what it was. Poor kid. Bella offered her the little room behind the pantry, but it was right by the back door and it made her nervous. The third floor's gross. I would have taken the pantry room in a heartbeat, but I didn't want to hurt Julee's and Maeve's feelings."

"Thanks. Off you go, then."

"I'll go get Cooper," Pete said as the door closed.

Demaris raised his hand. "Hold up. I know it's out of order, but let's grab Angie now. They'll need her during dinner, and I'm happy to bump Mr. Cooper for the time being."

Pete grinned. It was one of his boss's favorite strategies with difficult suspects, making them wait. "Doctor Cooper to you," he said, grabbing his jacket.

"Temperature's dropping," Bess said, shivering as they stood knee-deep in the rising tide. "I wonder how high the water gets in here at high tide?"

"Judging by the barnacles and seaweed, it fills up to the ceiling. Maybe we can grab on and pull ourselves up onto the path at high tide?"

"Over that overhang?"

"They'll find us before then, sweetie," Jane said, hugging her.

"Come on. Let's do a jog around the cave to keep warm while calling for help."

As Bess followed her friend, teeth chattering in the cold, she wondered if she'd ever see Roger again.

ANGIE SMITH'S BLACK PANTS AND CRISP WHITE UNIFORM SHIRT LOOKED two sizes too big. She sat down on the sofa, eyes darting around the room, finally coming to rest on her inquisitor. "Is this gonna take long? Chef's in a pissy mood, and I've got to get back."

Demaris smiled, taking the seat opposite her. "We'll have a word with Ms. Frey. This won't take long." He consulted his watch and was surprised to see it was after five.

"Can we get you anything to drink? Water? Tea? Soda?"

"No, thanks. I'm good."

"So, we're asking everyone about last night, where you were, what you were doing, and whether you saw or heard anything unusual. Can you tell us about your evening?"

"It's gonna sound lame, but after we finished work, Clara and I went to their private rooms behind the parlor and played cribbage. We both love to play."

"Did you know where the other young people were?"

"The guys went down to the beach to drink. They do that most nights. Clara and I don't drink, so we never go. Georgia does sometimes, but she's obsessed with her new boyfriend right now and spends hours talking and texting him every night. I'm pretty sure that's what she was doing because she left an empty soda can in my room. She goes in there so she can talk without Maeve and Julee listening. They share a room."

"So, Maeve and Julee had already retired then?"

She shrugged. "Maeve was probably asleep, but Julee might've still been in the kitchen. She preps after everyone leaves when it's quiet."

"Until what time?"

Another shrug. "I sometimes hear her coming up after midnight. I'm a light sleeper."

"Did you hear anything in the night? Someone reported hearing a scream."

"Not in the attic. I may sleep light, but sounds get pretty muffled once you get up to the third floor and shut the hall door."

"How well do you know your fellow workers?"

"I know them, but we're not exactly best buds. They pretty much ignore me. I'm invisible to everyone but Clara, and Georgia when she needs a favor. Then there was Daisy. She was great. I'll miss her."

"You knew her well, then?"

She lowered her gaze. "No... I mean, we were just starting to get friendly. I go to school with the guys and Georgia, so even though we don't exactly socialize, I'd seen Daisy and Scott with them around campus. I knew who she was."

"Then you'd become better acquainted here?"

"Sort of. As I said, I'm not in with those guys, and she didn't seem to be either. She was always making snippy comments about them."

"Like what?"

"That they were snotty and fake. Said that she and Scott stopped hanging out with them. She never said, but it seemed like they might have had a fight or something."

They chatted for a few more minutes before Demaris said, "That's all for now. Thanks, Angie. Detective Dugan will walk you back."

They stood together, and as she turned toward the door, he said, "One more thing. Someone saw Daisy out walking along the cliffs last night. Any idea who she might have been with? Did she tell you her evening plans?"

"No, but I think she was planning to spend time with her mom's boyfriend. She says...said...she liked him way more than her mom."

"Okay, then. We'll let you go."

When the door closed, he went to the kitchen and splashed water on his face. Hours of back-to-back interviews took their toll. His eyes stung, his back hurt, and he wished he could be out hiking with Jane and Bess instead of shut in the musty old cottage. He hoped she'd had a good afternoon and wished they could go home to their beautiful new house, just the two of them. While he waited for Pete's return, he grabbed his jacket and went out the back door for some fresh air, circling the cottage and sitting on a rickety rocker on the front porch to wait.

CHAPTER 20

"So do you have anything further to add Mr. Cooper?" Demaris asked. The supercilious professor and all his posturing had given him a headache. He had rambled on for twenty minutes saying that he couldn't think of anyone who would want to harm his precious girl, didn't know her friends, and had been home in bed in Greenleaf until he'd gotten the call from Fawn.

When queried about whether anyone could verify that he was home in bed, he hemmed and hawed before saying, "My wife and I are separated, okay? That's *my* dirty laundry. You satisfied? She just moved out last week and took our kids with her. So, I was alone last night. I did see my neighbor on my way out this morning if that helps.

"I don't know why you're grilling me. Talk to Robles. He's a sleazeball, and I've always thought he was inappropriate around Daise."

"In what way?"

"You know. Always sucking up to her, taking her out to 'dad and daughter' dinners. Like he was her father."

"And Fawn didn't object to this so-called inappropriateness?"

Cooper shrugged. "Who knows? Probably glad to have both of 'em out of her hair. She and Robles are on the outs, you know. I was keeping an eye out in case he suddenly tried to move in with Daisy. Wouldn't put it past the scumbag."

Demaris's head throbbed. He was pretty sure Cooper was lying, but had to follow through. "Have you any proof that something inappropriate was going on?"

"Do you mean was I in the bedroom with them? No."

"I think that's all," Demaris said. "Do we have your contact information in case we need to speak again?"

"Your sidekick there took it all down. I haven't decided whether to stay tonight, here or at the B and B in the village."

Pete opened the door and looked to his boss like he was ready to hurl the man out, when he paused. "That was a weird noise...like someone shrieking."

Cooper shook his head as if he was dealing with an imbecile. "Damn seagulls. They really get going at this time of day. Rats of the sea."

Pete gave his boss the eye, then said, "Ready, Mr. Cooper?"

"Thanks, Pete," Roger said, ignoring Jerry Cooper. "I texted Greta my dinner order. Let her know what you want and see how they're doing over there. When they're free, have them come back with the food."

"Will do," Pete said, waving Cooper to the open door.

"Guess I know when I'm dismissed," Cooper grumbled, as they stepped onto the porch.

Pete had just returned to the cottage and was sitting with his boss when the door slammed open, and the rest of the team burst in. Surprised, Demaris gazed from Greta to Brendan. "That was quick. here's the food?"

"They're missing," she said breathlessly. Both she and Stevens had clearly been running.

"Who?" he asked. Pete stood, ready for action.

"Jane and Bess. We expected them for their interviews a half an hour ago. No one's seen them since the afternoon workshop. According to Bella Vickers, they headed out for a walk a couple of hours ago."

Demaris stood, hand shaking as he grabbed his phone. He punched in a number, asked for Chief Smith, then requested every man his friend could spare to head over to the island. When he clicked off, he called the Old Harbor police station and made the same request of Chief Wilbur.

"Okay, let's go. I want every person you can find out looking for them."

"Even if one of them might be the killer?" Greta said.

"Insist people pair up for the search. You and Brendan alert everyone at the inn. No one's cooking or preparing dinner until they're found, understand? You two take the west path along the cliffs. Pete and I will go east from here. Ask Ron Vickers to meet the teams coming from Old Harbor and Mattapoisett. Chief Smith is sending five officers, Wilbur three. He'll have them fan out. Have Ron search every space in the inn, the barns, and the other cottage too."

Demaris grabbed his jacket and headed for the back door. "Call us if you hear anything," he shouted over his shoulder.

Pete glanced at Greta, then followed. "Let's hope they're sitting somewhere shooting the breeze," Pete said as he hurried to fall in beside his boss.

"How long ago was that scream?"

"Maybe fifteen minutes?" Pete said.

"That was no gull."

CHAPTER 21

Standing in chest-high water, Bess and Jane shivered, holding each other for warmth. "They'll find us," Bess whispered through chattering teeth. "They've just got to."

"Ready for another scream session?" Jane asked. "I think I can manage a short one without dying of cold," she said, before collapsing against her friend.

"Jane, wake up," Bess said, frantically shaking her. "Please wake up! Help! Help! Help!" she cried. "We're here! Please help us!"

As darkness descended, she struggled to hold her friend and keep her eyes open.

～

"Could you tell the direction of what you heard?" Roger asked Pete as the men hurried along the cliff path.

"Who knows with all the sounds of the ocean, but I think it was to the southeast." Pete glanced over at his boss. He was holding it together by a thread. If anyone else had gone missing, he'd probably have waited and conducted a quiet search. Hell, the island was the size of two or three football fields. They'd have covered it in a couple of hours.

In the past, Pete hadn't liked Bess, not because of any defect in her character, but because of the torment her existence wreaked on the man he loved like a father. Roger and Bess had been high school sweethearts. While he didn't know all the details, he knew that Rodge had been the cause of their breakup, not her. Despite this, his boss had never stopped loving the quiet, unassuming art teacher. Roger had suffered through her happy marriage to Mac Demaris, then stood by as she fell in love and engaged herself to Harry Winthrop. Now after two decades of watching Roger's agony, the couple was married and, from all indications, blissfully happy. *If he loses her now, we'll lose him,* Pete thought as they rounded a bend in the path.

His boss's gaze was northward, searching the tall field grass to their left. By default, Pete turned his attention to the water side and the profusion of beach roses and wild, scraggly bushes that lined the cliffs. As he studied the vegetation for any signs of human presence, something caught his eye: a patch of solid green amid the leaves and flowers. "Rodge, over here!" he called as he ran to the spot and pulled out a small woven backpack. As his boss approached, he opened the bag and pulled out a wallet. "Jane Fellows," he said, holding up the license. "This is her purse."

They began to peer into the bushes, making their way slowly until they reached an opening. "Bess! Jane!" Roger cried, peering downward. As they stepped farther in, off the path, they could hear water lapping against the cliff walls. Pete shone his flashlight downward. "Looks like some kind of a cave that's filling with water. There's a ledge, then ocean. Can't see over the rim."

"Call Greta and get someone to bring rope and warm blankets. If they're down there, they've got to be frozen. Bess! Jane!" he called over and over as he made his way downward along the edge of the slick rock pathway.

After speaking to Greta, Pete edged down the opposite side until they reached the rock overhang. "There they are, boss!" he cried. The other man slipped out of his shoes and hurled himself over the edge.

～

Strong arms lifted her, holding her and Jane above the water. "Roger, you found us!" she sputtered, spitting seawater as she held on for dear life. Her friend was unconscious, but alive.

From above, Pete secured his legs and feet around roots and branches as he leaned over, reaching down to pull first Jane, then Bess, over the ledge.

"Never mind me," Demaris said. "Get them up to high ground."

Once on solid ground, Bess rallied, her stiff cold arms and legs loosening up as she helped Pete with Jane. They'd gone less than two feet upward, Pete pulling from above, Bess pushing from below, clinging to branches and roots so as not to fall back over the ledge, when Jane coughed and sputtered, vomiting seawater and moaning. At the same moment, lights flashed from above and Stevens appeared, strapped into a rappelling harness.

"Where the hell did you get that rig?" Pete said, never so glad to see their youngest team member.

"Smith's guys had one in their truck. We can rope the two of them together and the guys and Greta will pull 'em up," Stevens said, unstrapping himself and handing the harness to Pete. "Where's the boss?"

"Below in the cave," Pete replied, calling down, "You okay, boss?"

"I'm okay, but a rope would be welcome once they're safe."

As soon as they strapped Jane and Bess into the harness, Pete turned to Stevens. "Take 'em up slowly, Brendan. I'm going back down."

Stevens nodded and gave the rope a sharp tug. As the three were pulled upward, Pete scrambled down and peered over the ledge again. His boss was treading water, lips blue, face pale and gray. "What the hell are you doing?" Demaris cried. "I told you to stay with her."

"They're safe with Brendan and Greta," Pete said. "Now let's get you outta there."

He wrapped his feet around roots and branches once again, then extended his arms downward. With a grimace, Demaris reached up, and they locked hands in a wrist hold. Slowly, Pete moved backward, through thorns and brambles, pulling him upward until Roger could gain a foothold and throw himself over the ledge.

"Jeez, am I glad you work out," he said, as Pete reached down to grasp his forearm.

As they made their way upward, Stevens appeared in the harness, and the three climbed the last bit together. As he stepped onto the path, Bess, wrapped in a blanket, threw herself at her husband.

"Roger, you're safe!" she cried, her body shaking with sobs.

Demaris held on for dear life, tears streaming down his face. Several minutes later, he looked up, meeting Greta's eyes. "Why didn't you take her back? Get her warm?"

"We tried, boss. She wouldn't go till you were out."

"Jane okay?"

"Seems so. They called a doctor, and Dr. Strauss is there waiting to help. Bella and Ron took her back so she could have a hot bath."

"Let's go, then," he said, still holding Bess close. "Can you walk, sweetheart?"

She nodded, and they set off toward the inn, Demaris barking orders to secure the area. "Soon as I get Bess to her room and change my clothes, I'll meet you back at the cottage. Shit, I don't have a change of clothes." He usually kept an emergency overnight bag in his truck, but Pete had driven.

Greta came up alongside them. "Boss, Ron Vickers said he'd lend you some things, and they'll wash and dry your clothes."

"Okay. Where's Brendan?"

"Here sir," Stevens said, appearing on their other side.

"You still got the harness?"

"Yes, sir."

"Good. Get your flashlight and go back down and grab my shoes. They're in the bushes on the left side of the path, just before the ledge. You and you," he said, pointing to two of Chief Smith's men. "Go with him. Work the ropes and stay until he's back up with my shoes."

They nodded and hurried back down the path with his junior officer.

CHAPTER 22

Once in the room, Bess insisted he shower first. She waited, huddled in a blanket and sitting in a desk chair until he emerged, a white towel wrapped around his waist. Clothes and his shoes had been delivered and awaited him on the bed. "I started the bath," he said, smiling. "I wish I could stay and scrub your back, or better still, hop in with you."

"Me too."

He dressed quickly, then came to hug her. "You're shivering, my love. The bath's nice and hot. In you go." He led to the bathroom and helped her peel off her wet clothes. After she settled in, letting out a sigh, he said, "I love you."

"I love you."

"I'll need to talk to you and Jane, after the doctor's come and gone. They're serving dinner downstairs. Are you up to that?"

"Of course."

"'Cause they'd bring you something up here if you'd rather?"

"Let me check with Jane. I'd like to be with her."

"There are officers posted outside both your doors."

She nodded. "I'll call her."

"Her cell phone's toast. It was in her bag, and someone stomped on it. When you're ready, the officer will take you down to her. Tell her I'll send someone into town for a temporary burner phone for her when I get downstairs. You sure you're okay?"

She nodded.

"After dinner, we'll come find you and Jane."

"It was deliberate, Roger. Someone pushed us down that path. Please be careful."

"Always, my love." He bent and kissed the top of her head, the wrench of stepping away physically painful. If he could, he'd never leave her side. Never. "And no more snooping. Someone's worried you're getting too close. That's likely why this happened."

She nodded.

"I mean this, Bess."

"I know."

He left without another word.

When Bess and Jane descended the steps to the parlor accompanied by one of Chief Smith's officers, they spied Hillary and Pete by the front door, arms wrapped around each other. It appeared that she did not want to let go. "I'm a phone call away, Hill. You'll be fine. Remember, don't go anywhere alone."

As Bess observed the couple, who had always seemed more like brother and sister, she caught a rare glimpse of Pete's soft side as he cupped his partner's face, kissing her forehead, then lips. "Love you, babe. I'll be back soon. Look, here are Bess and Jane," he added, stepping back. "Ron and I have to get this food to the team."

As Bess put her arm around Hillary's shoulders, Vickers handed Pete a large cardboard box, before taking a second one from his daughter. "I can take these over with Detective Dugan," Clara said, dressed in the now-familiar white shirt and black pants.

"Thanks, honey, but they need you in the dining room. Off you go." He turned to Bess and Jane. "You ladies okay?"

"Much improved. The wonders of a hot bath," Jane replied.

"We better get going," Pete said. "Someone will come and get you during dinner. We'll text first."

"Thanks, Pete," Bess said, and the men headed off.

THE MOMENT JANE AND BESS STEPPED INTO THE DINING ROOM, THEY were besieged by authors and staff alike. Marilyn rushed them with air kisses, Nancy behind her, smiling and asking how they were. Claire and Yorky waved at them from across the room.

Bess turned to Hillary. "You coming?"

"I better check in with the sisters," Hillary said. "Ashlyn texted a little while ago begging me to join them. I know she loves her sister, but I get the impression they don't hang out together very often."

"What about their book collaborations?"

"Mostly done electronically. You ladies okay?"

"Yes, fine," Bess said. "Enjoy your dinner."

"How are you?" Claire asked, taking Bess's hand as she sat beside her. "Yorky and I have been so worried since we heard. How terrifying for you."

Bess smiled at her, then him. "Thanks, we're fine, but I wouldn't want to repeat it again."

"Glad you're both safe," Yorky said, holding Jane's gaze a bit longer. He had taken wonderful care of her earlier before the doctor's arrival.

Bob Franklin sat down across the table. His blue eyes sparkled with warmth as he nodded at Bess and Jane. "Glad to see you ladies looking so well."

"Thanks, Bob," Jane said as Angie appeared, water pitcher in hand.

"Oh, Ms. Demaris, Ms. Fellows, are you okay? The staff's been freaked!"

"We're fine, Angie. No worries," Bess said, looking up at her. Angie did look genuinely stricken, her eyes darting from Jane to her.

"I feel so bad. I was gonna hike around the island on my break, but I wasn't sure I'd be back in time for my interview. I could have helped you."

"We're fine," Jane said. "And very hungry. What are the specials tonight?"

As they chatted over appetizers, Fawn and Kyle strolled in and joined Marilyn, Nancy Beck, and Leo Tallstory. Jerry Cooper trailed behind them. No sign of Wilma Conlon. Bess decided that if she appeared, they'd squeeze Wilma in at their table rather than subjecting her to that bunch. As the group sat, Jade stood and rushed toward the French doors.

"Wonder where she's off to?" Jane whispered.

"Poor thing," Claire said. "This afternoon has been frightening for all of us. We've all walked along the cliffs. What happened to you two could have happened to any one of us."

Bess watched as Angie intercepted Jade and attempted to comfort her, only to be rebuffed. Jade pushed her away and disappeared. *There's another poor thing,* she thought. *Everyone's always brushing by her like she's invisible.*

CHAPTER 23

Demaris gazed around at his team, a smile on his face. He was damn lucky, and he knew it. He tried never to take them for granted. Pete had been with him for seventeen years, Greta since the establishment of RHD, and Brendan almost two years.

Gathered around the cottage table, the four were enjoying another delicious meal. All but Brendan had ordered the evening's special, fisherman's stew served with garlic bread and a crisp field greens salad. Brimming with scallops, fish, lobster, and littlenecks, the tomato-based garlicky broth was sublime.

Greta groaned. "Too bad we're on duty. All this needs is a glass of wine and I'd be in heaven. Do you think they gave us enough bread to sop up all this amazing broth?"

Demaris chuckled, marveling as he always did at how much food his petite detective managed to consume. "There's another bag of bread down there," he said, pointing to the end of the table. "How's your burger, Brendan?"

"Great, sir. Wish I could eat seafood. That looks incredible."

"You don't like any seafood?" his boss asked.

His young officer grinned. "Do fish sticks count? I'm allergic to most seafood, so I usually don't take the chance."

Demaris grabbed his napkin, then shuffled a pile of notes to the left of his plate. "Let's get started, okay? Anyone mind if we talk while we eat?"

"Is Burke capable of that?" Pete asked as his colleague, grabbed another hunk of bread. Greta's appetite was legendary.

"Ha-ha," she said, then set the bread at the edge of her plate and took up her notes.

His plate clean, Brendan followed suit and slid his iPad nearer.

"Keep eating, everyone. Let's hear from Greta and Brendan first, then plan our next moves. We haven't completed the initial interviews. I know Greta and Brendan still have the caretaker and the cook. Anyone else?"

"Beck Bailey," she replied through a mouthful of bread. "He was taking a nap when we went to grab him, and his wife refused to wake him up."

"Okay, then. We still have a couple of the waitstaff, Gus Wilkins and Henry Lewis. I'd also like to check in with Kyle Robles. See where he was after the afternoon workshop. It would take strength… what happened on the cliff." He swallowed, unable to give name to the incident that almost killed his wife. "After Robles, we'll bring Bess and Jane over for their account."

"Can we help with any of that?" Greta asked.

"Thanks, but we're all set. My gut tells me the caretaker, George Whipple, isn't involved in any of this, but better to be thorough. You can catch him tonight or tomorrow morning."

"Sure thing," Greta said.

"It's my preference that we all spend the night here. Is that a problem for anyone? Greta, can you get coverage for your mom?"

She nodded. "She's got a caretaker twenty-four-seven now. My brother arranged it, and he foots the bill." Her mother's health had been failing for years. Wheelchair-bound, Wilma Burke had emphysema and the beginnings of dementia.

"You're able to stay, then?"

She nodded. "Yes, boss."

"Brendan, how about you?"

"Of course, sir."

"Good. You two can bunk out here, and Pete and I will stay with Hillary and Bess. I've got one of Smith's men ready to drive Brendan to RHD to pick up my truck. I keep a change of clothes in the truck. On your way back, stop in at the tech place on Northport Pike. They're open till ten. Grab two burner phones, an extra and one for Ms. Fellows until she can replace her phone."

"Yes, sir."

"Greta, you okay interviewing on your own until Brendan gets back?"

"Yes, boss."

"I wonder how dinner's going?" Pete said.

"We'll know soon when we start grabbing people," Demaris said.

Greta eyed her bowl and pulled another hunk of bread from the loaf. "Should we tell people to stay close to the inn or in their rooms?"

"According to the leaders, everyone should be participating in their smaller critique groups. Marilyn and Nancy thought it'd be best to keep them occupied."

"And all together so they can't get into any more trouble," Pete said.

Demaris gazed over at his second-in-command, a slight grin on his face. "Something like that. We'll find out where these groups are meeting and snatch people as needed. Same with the staff. Greta, take it away."

CHAPTER 24

Greta set down her fork and turned to her boss. "Okay, well, Julee Frey is a talented chef, but she didn't impress me as a murderer, right, Brendan?"

Brendan nodded, wiping his napkin over his iPad.

Greta flipped through her notebook then set it aside. "She's been working for the Vickerses for years. Bella and Ron Vickers confirmed this. Both Bella and Ron have met Fawn Davis and Robles previously because Fawn's taught yoga at several retreats here over the years. Daisy had never come with them, and Robles was merely a hanger-on, never a presenter. Claimed to anyone who'd listen that he was retreating to focus on his writing. Julee isn't too impressed with him."

"Join the club," Pete muttered.

"Where was Ms. Frey this afternoon?"

"She took a nap, then spent most of her time in the kitchen. Same with the housekeeper Maeve Carney. When we asked both about their whereabouts, they had pretty much the identical story—nap, then work. People were in and out as they did their thing. Carney seems to spend most of her running around supervising the maids and busboys. Says they're all lazy kids except for Angie."

"Sounds like there's a lot of napping around here," Roger said. "Thanks for grabbing Carney. Pete and I ran out of time."

"No problem, boss." Greta looked longingly at remnants of her dinner, then continued. "Carney's worked here for three years in the summer months. Knows Fawn from her yoga classes, same as Julee. She's participated in Fawn's classes here and in Providence."

"That's where she's from?" Roger asked.

Greta nodded. "She's actually pretty friendly with Fawn, but claims she downplays it here 'cause she doesn't want to be unprofessional. Like that matters in this context."

"What about Daisy?"

"Knew her, thinks she was a spoiled brat, but doesn't know anyone who'd want to harm her. Didn't seem to know Robles or Jerry Cooper, although when Brendan and I came upon her unexpectedly, she was locked in what looked like a very friendly conversation with Cooper."

Roger made a note to speak to Carney and Cooper in the morning. "So, the housekeeper has hidden depths."

"Appears so," Greta replied, taking advantage of the slight pause to sop up the rest of her broth.

"So, who else?"

"We talked with Dr. Strauss before Bess and Jane disappeared. His whereabouts were accounted for all day today. During Daisy's murder, says he was fast asleep. Claims to be a very sound sleeper. Ms. Rubin confirmed his whereabouts today, except when the two of them went to their rooms after the Bailey workshop to—you guessed it—take a nap. He had never met Fawn or Daisy prior to this week and didn't offer an opinion on either. Seems like a genuinely nice man. He and Ms. Rubin seem to have a thing going."

Her boss nodded.

"My gut tells me he's not our guy," she added.

"Never know," Pete said, leaning back in his chair. "Sometimes it's the nice guys." He made a gesture like a knife slitting across his neck.

Demaris ignored him. "What about the others?"

"Marilyn and Beck know the Davis-Robles clan well. They all live in Providence, she takes Fawn's yoga classes, and they all belong to a meditation sangha on the East Side."

"Bailey too?" Demaris asked.

Pete dropped the front legs of his chair back on the floor with a thud. "What's a sangha?"

"I had to ask too," Brendan said, gazing over at his hero in a rare instance of him speaking without being asked to do so by his superiors. "It's a spiritual group that meets to meditate."

Pete rolled his eyes. "Hill wanted to join a meditation group in Old Harbor. Sounds boring."

"It isn't," his boss said, then turned back to Greta. "Go on, please."

"The couples socialize, and the Baileys have two offspring, ages nineteen and twenty. The kids hang out once in a while, and they've taken a couple of family vacations together. Both Bailey and Lively said their kids weren't close to Daisy. Claimed they hadn't seen her in ages. I got the impression there was more to their story, especially between Marilyn and Robles."

Demaris met her eyes. "Oh, in what way?"

"Just a gut feeling. Every time Robles's name came up, she twitched, and Beck looked down at the floor. Weird."

"How about Nancy Pratt?"

"She and Marilyn are in the same Rhode Island writers' group. They've been friendly for years. She didn't know Daisy and Fawn and was noncommittal about Robles. She's probably the most successful author here this week, despite all Kyle's puffery, Marilyn's overinflated ego, and Tallstory's horn tooting. Nancy has four very successful romantic suspense series. Well written."

Demaris smiled. "You're a fan, then?"

Greta grinned. "As a matter of fact, I am."

Demaris scratched his head, smiling at her. "I'll have to try one, I guess. So, what about the mystery-writing sisters?"

"Ashlyn, the older one, appears relatively normal, but Jade seems a bit odd. They both grew up in Greenleaf. Still live there now. Father's an English professor at the college. Ashlyn's married to Jared Fields. He's a journalist for the *New York Times*, constantly traveling around the world. Jade's single. Neither of them knew Daisy or Fawn.

They do know Jerry Cooper, and we got the feeling he's not high on their list of favorite people.

"They were in bed asleep when Daisy was murdered. They're sharing a room. Jade takes heavy-duty sleep pills. Claims to have heard nothing in the night. Same with Ashlyn. After Beck Bailey's workshop, they spent the time before dinner writing in their room. Hillary joined them for most of the time. They wrote for an hour or so, then shared. Not sure how that works with the sisters writing the same book, but they didn't elaborate. We asked Hillary about them, and she confirmed their whereabouts."

Greta looked over at Pete. "Hill might have more insights or information about them if you can check tonight? Every time Kyle Robles or Jerry Cooper was mentioned, Jade seemed to blanch, didn't she, Brendan?"

Stevens nodded. "She kinda did, sir. She's also anorexic and bulimic. My cousin suffers from that, and Ms. Temple has all the signs, including having to excuse herself at one point to throw up her lunch."

"Terrible affliction," Demaris said. "See if you can learn when her illness began."

Greta nodded.

"Okay, then. I think that's enough for now. Let's everyone hit it, see if we can complete interviews during tonight's critique groups, then stay visible till everyone's tucked into in bed." He looked from Greta to Stevens. "You two got everything you need out here?"

They both nodded.

"Okay, let's bring the dirty dishes over. Save the staff a trip."

CHAPTER 25

"What the hell is this?" Robles asked, slamming into the cottage, the door banging against the wall, Pete trailing behind him.

"Mr. Robles, thank you for joining us. This shouldn't take too long, and you can get back to your dinner."

"Screw you. This is harassment. What the hell could I possibly tell you that I haven't already?"

"Why don't we start with a fuller accounting of your relationship with Daisy Davis."

"Excuse me?"

"Then we can talk about your whereabouts this afternoon."

"I don't know who's been feeding you lies, but my relationship with Daisy was simply a father-daughter one. She and her mom didn't get along, so when she was home, I tried to smooth things over, give her a little attention."

"Did Daisy grow resentful of your attentions and push you away? Reject your advances?"

"There were no advances! Besides, the last year or so, she was always with Scott. The three of us would hang out sometimes. I'd go down to Bell Haven or we'd do something in Providence. I always asked Fawn to come along, but she usually declined. She's kind of an introvert when she's not teaching."

"And where were you this afternoon?"

"I went to Bailey's boring workshop. Waste of time. Then I went back to the suite for a nap. Fawn was there with Mr. Pompous Dickhead Cooper hovering over her like she was on death's door."

"Was Mr. Cooper with her all afternoon, then?"

"Far as I know. He wasn't at the workshop, so I figured he was with Fawn."

They talked for a few more minutes, then Pete stood to escort Robles back to the inn and retrieve Bess and Jane. Once dismissed, Robles slammed out the door without a word. Pete followed him, waving to his boss over his shoulder.

Roger closed his eyes, breathing slowly and hoping to stave off a full-blown migraine.

GRETA MOVED ABOUT, CANVASSING AND REINTERVIEWING PEOPLE ABOUT their whereabouts after Beck Bailey's workshop, Brendan joined her upon his return with Demaris's clothes and truck. Roger and Pete sat down with Bess and Jane.

The two friends sat opposite him, side by side on the love seat, Pete in a chair off to one side.

"How are you ladies doing?"

"Warm at last, but pissed," Jane replied. "We could have died down there."

Demaris swallowed hard, the lump still lodged in his throat since hearing they were missing. "And we will catch the person responsible. Is there anything you remember about the person or persons?"

"It was definitely one person," Bess said.

Jane turned to her, a surprised look in her eyes. "How can you be sure?"

"It just felt like that, momentum-wise, their right hand on me, left on you," Bess said.

"Any sense of the size of the hand? Large? Small and delicate?"

"I'm pretty sure he or she was wearing gloves," his wife replied. "I caught just a brief flash of light brown leather before the shove."

"Work gloves?" Demaris asked.

"Something like that."

Jane nodded. "She's right. There's was a kind of rough feel on the small of my back."

"Did the person speak or make any kind of noise?"

"Not that I recall," Bess said.

"Smell? Did you get a whiff of him or her?"

Both women shook their heads. After describing their fall, they spent a few minutes describing their day and their conversations with "suspects," as Jane referred to them. Demaris held his temper, inwardly furious at them for getting involved. His blood ran cold when he thought how close to losing Bess he'd come.

"Okay, then. The team is working through the dinner hour and your critique groups, then we'll all be at the inn watching over things. The kitchen's keeping your dinners warm. Pete'll take you back." Demaris stood and walked them to the door, embracing his wife and planting a kiss on her temple. "See you later."

She smiled at him, touching his cheek. "Yes."

As they strolled back to the inn, Jane gazed over at Pete. "Ordinarily, I'd have bristled at needing an escort, but after today, I'm sure glad to have our bodyguard at our side."

He grinned. "You're safe now, and there'll be an officer posted outside your door all night."

"Thanks," Jane replied, taking his arm.

CHAPTER 26

Most people's dinners had been cleared away by the time Bess and Jane sat down. Soon after their arrival, Bob excused himself to prepare for his critique group, but Claire and Yorky remained, sipping their coffees. Hillary, Jade, and Ashlyn were playing cards in the parlor, and Wilma Conlon was nowhere to be seen. They had just settled in when Angie appeared with their dinners, kept warm under stainless steel plates covers, which she removed with a flourish.

Bess gazed up at her. "This looks amazing, Angie."

"Aside from tonight's fisherman's stew, pasta is one of Chef's specialties. She makes it from scratch, with help from us, and her sauces are to die for."

Bess had ordered mushroom ravioli made with five varieties of fresh mushrooms and a sauce loaded with more mushrooms. Jane had ordered lobster ravioli in a pink sauce with chunks of lobster meat on top. They both had field greens on the side, and Angie set down a basket of crusty bread between them.

"Anything else I can get you ladies?" Angie asked.

"I'd like a huge glass of Pinot Noir. Huge," Jane said.

"And I'd love a glass of your house white," Bess said.

"It changes every night," Angie said. "They're featuring a local Pinot Grigio tonight."

"Perfect," Bess said.

"Wait," Jane called. "I know this is going to sound strange, but can you bring unopened bottles of both wines and pour them at the table? I'm happy to pay for this."

"No problem, of course," Angie said, eyes wide as saucers. "After what you've been through, I can see how you'd want that. I doubt the Vickerses will charge extra either."

She disappeared, and five minutes later, Gus Wilkins appeared with glasses, both wine bottles, and a corkscrew. For some reason, he had been designated as sommelier whenever anyone requested wine be opened at the table.

Tall and lean with tussled blond hair, he was good-looking, and he knew it. He gave the two friends an insouciant expression, hazel eyes peering down at them. "Who's the red?"

Jane frowned. "I'm not a bottle of wine, thank you, but I did order the Pinot Noir."

Ignoring her sarcasm, he uncorked and poured both wines, waited for their approval, then popped the corkscrew into his vest pocket. The vest was black leather, and he was the only member of the waitstaff who wore one. After he headed to the kitchen to fetch an ice bucket for the white wine, Jane muttered, "Obnoxious little prick."

Bess elbowed her. "Shush."

"Just because he's wearing that shiny biker vest doesn't mean he's better than the others. I'm surprised Ron and Bella allow it."

"Here he comes," Claire whispered as Gus approached with the ice bucket and stand, which he set at Bess's side.

"So, what's your story, Gus?" Jane asked. "Is this your first summer here?"

He guffawed. "Hardly. I live on the island. There are a couple of houses on the other side. I rent one with a couple of buddies. I've been working for the Vickerses in the summers for years."

"So, you live here year-round?" Bess asked.

"Yup."

"No college?" Yorky asked.

"Two years and that was enough for me. I can do my job anywhere."

Bess looked up. "Which is?"

"I'm a techie. I take on large-scale projects for customers. All kinds of things."

Bess wanted to query further, but decided no more snooping, at least for tonight.

"Where'd you go to college?" Yorky asked.

Gus paused, then said, "Greenleaf."

"So, you know the other staff from there?" Jane asked.

"I know 'em. Georgia and I hung out freshman year. Nothing serious, ancient history. None of us are best buds or anything. Now, is that all? I've gotta get back to the kitchen."

"He's full of himself," Claire whispered, as Gus strolled off.

Bess nodded. "Full of himself, yes. He'd also know the island and all its nooks and crannies, wouldn't he?"

"Absolutely," Jane said. "And if he's Georgia's age, their history can't be too ancient. And years? We... I mean, Roger should find out from Ron and Bella how long he's been working for them."

Ten minutes later, Marilyn stood, the sound of tinkling reaching them as she tapped her water glass with a spoon. "Good evening, everyone. I trust you enjoyed a wonderful dinner. Sorry to interrupt, but the evening critique groups will begin in twenty minutes. This should give Bess and Jane time to savor their meals. Each group will meet in their usual space. Bess and Jane, I wonder if you'd mind bringing your dessert and coffee to your meetings? I'm sure you're tired, as we all are, after the events of today. It will be good to get an early start, then have an early night. Tomorrow morning, Nancy and I will present a workshop on writing series, then the plan is to group up again in the afternoon."

Yorky raised his hand.

"Yes, Dr. Strauss?" she said.

"What are the plans after tomorrow afternoon?"

"We're taking a wait-and-see approach until the police let us know when we can leave the island. As you know, we have two more days of the retreat, but I'm sensing people's hearts aren't into staying if they're allowed to go home."

Claire raised her hand. "What about the agent and editor meetings?"

"We promise to decide about those meetings and the retreat's last day's activities by the conclusion of afternoon groups tomorrow. Enjoy your evening, if that's possible," she concluded, then swished from the room, Beck and Nancy following in her wake.

"Yeah, right," Jane said, forking a luscious bite of ravioli.

"I wonder where Wilma is," Bess said. "I haven't seen her since Beck's workshop."

"Bella told me she requested dinner in her room," Claire said. "I think the day's events really shook her up."

"Poor Wilma," Bess said, thinking about the diminutive librarian on whom she depended for her reading choices. Any book Wilma recommended was perfect. She knew her patrons, their likes, dislikes, and favorite authors. Her special interest was mysteries. As far as Bess could tell, there wasn't a mystery Wilma hadn't read.

"Hope she's okay," Jane said, echoing Bess's thoughts.

Bess nodded. "I think I'll ask Pete or one of the others to check on her."

CHAPTER 27

"Are you okay?" Roger asked as he brushed strands of hair from Bess's cheek. They lay in their comfortable bed, covered with eiderdowns.

"Now, I am," she murmured as she snuggled closer.

"I wish I could take you home now, away from all this."

"Have you gotten anywhere?"

He shook his head.

"Why would anyone want to harm Jane and me?"

He pulled the pillows up behind him and sat up, his arm still wrapped around her. "Could be a psycho who strikes out indiscriminately, or it might have been to warn us off. My guess is you two asked a few too many questions."

"But we—"

"Save it Bess. I love you, but you and Jane have got to stop. I warned you not to get involved in this."

She opened her mouth to protest, then simply said, "Pete said something, didn't he?"

"Yes. When you came for your interview, I had intended to give you a stern lecture. Then all hell broke loose."

"We were just trying to help."

"I know, but it's dangerous."

"For you too."

He smiled, leaning down to kiss her. "Yes, but unlike you, I have my bulldog watching my back, and he's armed."

"I just want it to end. I hope you find the person soon. I've learned some useful writing tips these past few days, but I'm ready to go home."

"Me too." He reached over and turned off the light. "Sleep well, my darling."

"Three more things. Leo Tallstory was acting strangely tonight in our critique group."

The light snapped back on. "How so?"

"He's usually very talkative, always interrupting and turning the conversation to his work, ignoring the rest of us, but he barely said a word tonight. He kept looking around like he was expecting some-one. Just wasn't like him."

"We'll have a chat with him in the morning. What're the other things?"

"Well...when Gus Wilkins was serving us tonight, he claimed to have been working for the Vickerses for years. It might be worth checking with Bella and Ron."

"We have. He's like a son to them. Birth parents were drug addicts. He's been in and out of foster care his whole life. Started working out here at thirteen. When he dropped out of Greenleaf, the Vickerses helped find him the house to rent on the other side of the island."

"Why doesn't he live there now?" Bess asked.

"Summer rentals. He just moved over here last week for the season. The first tenants arrive next week."

"What about the other houses on the island?"

"Empty. No heat. They've been searched. So, what else?"

"Well... Angie told us, and I assume you know, that five of the staff kids are adoptees. Daisy and Angie, of course, but also Matt, Henry, and Georgia. Then there's Gus."

"Who was never adopted. Matt's parents died young, and he was adopted by his aunt and uncle. Henry's parents couldn't conceive and used a surrogate. Georgia was adopted through a reputable agency and has a paper trail that leads back to her birth mother, who became pregnant at fifteen and gave her up for adoption."

"Very thorough background checks," she said.

"Stevens and Greta. They're both incredible researchers, especially Brendan, although I'd never tell Greta." Once again, he reached for the light. "No more items?"

"No," she said, drawing closer, loving the feel of his warm body against her. "That's it."

"And no more sleuthing for you."

They fell asleep wrapped in each other's arms.

Safe, he thought as he drifted off.

KNOCKING WOKE THEM LESS THAN AN HOUR LATER. "STAY HERE," ROGER whispered, grabbing one of the inn's fluffy white robes.

When he opened the door, he found Pete dressed in an identical outfit. "Sorry, boss. Can I come in for a sec? Didn't think I should wait till morning."

Roger turned to check on Bess, who was now robed and sitting up in bed, then stepped aside. "We can talk over here," he said, indicating the small sitting area near the windows with a view of the dark ocean below. Absently noticing that the drapes were open, he moved to close them, then took one of the two chairs covered in faded blue denim. "Shoot."

"Just as we were going to...well, I mean, we were in bed and—"

"I get the picture, Pete. Out with it."

"Well, Hill says out of the blue, 'There's something odd about her.' So much for romance, I thought. Sat up, turned on the light, and she starts telling me how weird Jade is. Says she's always staring off into space and her sister has to snap her fingers like she's bringing her out of a trance or something. The other thing she does is ramble on about stuff, abruptly changing the subject. You know?"

"What kind of stuff?"

"Random stuff, according to Hillary. She said that when they sat down at lunch today, Jade went into one of her trances. When Hill asked what was the matter, she whispered, 'He raped me. He's gonna do it again. I can tell. When he recognizes me, he's gonna do it again. Have to stop him, have to stop him.'"

Hill said that Jade was staring at the table with all the hoity-toities. You know, Marilyn Lively and her husband, the Tallstory guy, Robles, and that jerk Jerry Cooper. Hill couldn't tell who she was looking at, and before she could ask, Jade stood and bolted out of the room."

"Yes, she did," Bess said. "Sorry, I overheard you. We all wondered about Jade, but it slipped my mind to mention it when we were talking earlier."

"Right," Roger said. "This is what we're going to do. We can't question Ms. Temple at this time of night, but let's call over to Brendan, and I'll call Chief Smith. One or two of his men and Brendan can take turns in the hall outside her room. If she comes out, tell them to request that she and her sister stay put until breakfast. Okay?"

"Sure, boss. Sorry to wake you."

"Glad you did. Take care."

Demaris phoned Paul Smith and got his assurance that one of his officers would be there in ten minutes. Then he turned to Bess. "I'll be back soon, my love. Just want to be sure Brendan's in place outside Jade's door. It's right down the hall, so we'll keep an eye on your door too. Get some sleep."

CHAPTER 28

Up at five thirty, Demaris dressed quickly. He was surprised to find Bess dressed in a sweatshirt and yoga pants when he emerged from the bathroom. "Are you going somewhere?"

"Meeting Jane for yoga. Fawn is holding the class in the parlor. Says she couldn't bear to step into the barn studio, but she still wants to stretch a bit."

"Now?"

"Apparently, Kyle is handling all the funeral arrangements as she 'can't cope with it.' She's kind of a weird person, if you ask me, but she's a wonderful yoga instructor."

He shrugged. "Everyone handles grief in their own way."

Bess met his eyes. "You have a soft spot for her, don't you?"

"Not sure it's a soft spot, but Fawn and others pulled me out of the abyss at a tough time in my life. I owe her. And I don't think she killed her daughter, despite their adversarial relationship."

"Daisy was a bit of a brat."

"Yes," he said, hugging and kissing her. "Gotta run."

With a last look at the person he loved, and had always loved, more than life itself, he opened the door and closed it, heading down to check on Brendan.

He found Stevens on duty, alert and wide awake in a straight-back chair that afforded a clear view of Jade and Ashlyn's door. As soon as the young officer saw him, he popped up, a wide grin on his face. "Good morning, sir."

"How's it going, Brendan? Are you exhausted?"

"No, sir. Fine, sir. I only took over an hour ago. Mattapoisett guys were here most of the night. Chief Smith sent two of his officers."

"Good work, thanks. This is what I want you to do. I'm gonna grab Pete and then talk to Maeve Carney and Jerry Cooper before breakfast. Do we know where Cooper's staying?"

"The Vickerses put him in a spare bedroom in their quarters. Nice of them."

"Okay, then. Do not let the sisters out of the room unless they'd both like to go to yoga class. If only Ms. Fields goes, stay here and monitor Ms. Temple. If they both go, please accompany them to the west parlor. Apparently, Ms. Davis is teaching a class there this morning."

Steven's face registered surprise.

"Yeah, seems strange, but sometimes it's better to keep busy at times like these. Especially when you've got Kyle Robles and Jerry Cooper hovering over you. Greta will also be on duty downstairs, so she can help you."

Stevens smiled. "Yes, sir."

"When Pete and I are finished with the Carney woman and Cooper, we'll text or call, and you can bring Ms. Temple to the cottage, okay?"

"Yes, sir."

"And, Brendan?"

"Yes, sir?"

"Don't let Jade Temple out of your sight."

THEY FOUND MAEVE CARNEY IN THE KITCHEN CHATTING WITH JULEE Frey, the latter wearing oven mitts as she removed pans of scones and muffins from the three ovens. The air, redolent with the scents of cinnamon, ginger, chocolate, and freshy baked bread, was intoxicating. "Morning, ladies," Demaris said. "Something smells delicious."

"Would you like one?" Julee asked, her pale blue eyes looking up from her work, curly red hair stuffed under a baseball cap. The hat, her hair, and her face were dusted with flour, her jeans too. She wore a long white chef's apron already dotted with what appeared to be jam. Julee was what one might call a solid woman. Of medium height, she had strong muscular arms honed by years of kneading dough and hefting heavy cookware. In comparison, her companion was rather plain, dressed as if she were auditioning for the part of Mrs. Danvers in DuMaurier's *Rebecca.* Slender, with brown hair pulled back in a bun, Maeve had dull gray eyes set in an oval face. Her eyes matched the color of her gray cotton dress, over which she wore an old-fashioned pinafore.

He smiled. "Thanks, but not right now. But I know what I'll order for breakfast." He turned to Maeve. "Ms. Carney, might we have a word?"

"Of course," she said. He opened the kitchen door leading to the back porch and a warm sunny morning. They strolled around to a quiet spot and sat in rockers pulled into a circle. "How can I help?" she asked, her voice calm and controlled.

Too controlled, too calm, Demaris thought. "I wanted to ask you about your interview with Detective Burke."

"Yes?"

"You indicated that you didn't know Jerry Cooper, yet my officers observed you two chatting, and you looked very friendly."

"I'm an employee here, Lieutenant. I'm paid to be friendly."

"It didn't look like that kind of friendly to them."

"And they're experts on the roles of a housekeeper, are they?"

"They're trained to read people. They're very good at their jobs, and I trust their insights and observations. We're in the middle of a homicide investigation, and there's a killer in our midst who might indeed kill again. I need for you to be forthcoming now, Ms. Carney."

"Fine, I know Jerry. So what? It has nothing to do with any of this, so I didn't think it was worth mentioning."

"If you were asked directly about someone or something, it is worth mentioning. How do you know Mr. Cooper?"

"If you must know, Jerry and I dated briefly. About ten years ago. Long after his affair with Fawn."

"How did you meet?"

"I took a course from him over six weeks in the summer. Since the course was filled with young coeds, we hooked up for coffee after class one day. That's how it started. It was very brief. Only a few short weeks, until I discovered he was married and broke it off. The break was amicable. We hardly knew each other. No hard feelings. Over the years, we've exchanged the occasional email, but I hadn't set eyes on him again till yesterday. It was good to see him."

"When you were dating, did he ever mention Fawn or Daisy Davis?"

"Of course not! As I just said, we barely knew each other. Why would he divulge something like that?"

"Well, thank you," Demaris said. "We'll let you get on with your work."

Carney quickly hurried off as the men rearranged the rockers and headed around the porch to the front door.

"No hard feelings, my eye," Demaris said. "I'll be interested to hear Mr. Cooper's version of this brief affair. Jerry does get around, doesn't he? I'd bet big money that he's had dozens of dalliances over the years."

"Sleazeball," Pete said, shaking his head. "And what's with Carney's getup? Not something you see every day. Who wears clothes like that anymore?"

Demaris shrugged, grinning. "Apparently housekeepers in remote scary hotels."

As they closed the front door, they gazed around and spied Jerry Cooper through the glass French doors leading to the west parlor. He was holding the downward dog position none too steadily. "You grab him. I want to talk to Ron Vickers," Demaris said. "Meet you back on the porch."

After speaking to Ron and ascertaining that Jerry Cooper had stayed put all night, Demaris joined Pete and a very irate Jerry Cooper on the porch. Beet red, he was ranting about their harassment. Pete had placed three rockers in a circle on the back porch. "Now you look here, you," Cooper said as Demaris appeared. "I've had just about enough! I could be home right now, out of your reach, and your prurient curiosity about my past."

"As it happens, Mr. Cooper, that is exactly what we want to be clear about, your less than admirable past. Sit!"

Cooper sat and faced the two men. "It's Dr. Cooper. So, what is it this time?"

"Let's start with your affair with Maeve Carney and go from there."

"Maeve? Don't be absurd. It was a summer dalliance. A bit of fun between two consenting adults. Maeve's a great gal."

"Where were your wife and family during this bit of fun?"

"None of your business!"

"I can get the exact dates from Ms. Carney and then check with your wife, if that's easier. In fact, if we don't get full cooperation from you right now, this minute, I'll send two of my officers to Greenleaf to chat with Ms. Cooper."

"You wouldn't dare."

"Try me."

"Fine. What do you want to know? Maeve and I are friends. We spent a couple of nice weeks together while Sara and the kids were visiting her family in North Carolina. I didn't go because I was teaching. Hell, people get lonely. It was the decade of free love. Everyone was screwing around in those days. Even the visiting profs were sleeping around. Take Bailey, for instance. He was one of the worst offenders. Always had something goin' on. I think he used his summer teaching to make his own private love connections."

"Excuse me?"

"Ol' Beck was pretty randy in his day."

"What about his wife?"

"She never came with him. Might show up for the occasional weekend, but she was usually off on some trip, book tour or travels with her women friends. If you haven't noticed, Beck's completely emasculated around Marilyn."

Demaris made a note to talk to Becker. "Let's get back to you, Dr. Cooper, shall we?

So, your wife never knew about the affair with Ms. Carney?"

"No, I love Sara. I didn't want to hurt her. No need. Maeve and I were over when my family returned."

"Okay, let's go a few years further back."

"Geez, here we go. Fawn again? What could I possibly add, especially since she and I have stayed friends?"

"I'm referring to the time about seventeen years ago when you raped your colleague's daughter, a crime for which you can still be prosecuted."

"What the hell are you talking about?"

"Jade Temple."

"That was consensual. She came on to me."

"She was fifteen."

"A very mature fifteen."

"We'll be getting Ms. Temple's version of the event later. If your so-called consensual liaison proves to be assault, we'll be taking you into custody."

"Now hold on."

"That's it for now, Mr. Cooper. You can return to your yoga class."

"But—"

"You're dismissed. Detective Dugan and I have work to do."

After staring at them dumbfounded for a moment or two, Cooper stalked off, and Demaris turned to Pete. "Call Brendan and tell him to get Jade to the cottage. She's not in the yoga class. Now. Wait at the front door for them and bring them over. Don't let Cooper near her, and keep her away from anyone, including her sister, okay? I'm heading over to check my notes."

"What's wrong with these people?" Pete said.

"Don't know. Assholes, the lot of them. This case is giving me a massive headache. See you soon."

As he headed to the porch steps, Demaris glanced inside the front windows and saw that the yoga class was breaking up. He spied Jane and Bess arm in arm and breathed a sigh of relief. *Safe.*

CHAPTER 29

"Jade, thanks for coming over."

Demaris gestured to the love seat, inviting her to sit. Her black tunic and yoga pants hung on her skeletal frame, her unwashed hair hanging limp around her shoulders. Her beautiful brown eyes looked sunken, dark circles under them as if she hadn't slept in days and had lost ten pounds since they'd first met her. "I promise not to keep you long. Can we offer you something to eat or drink? A nice basket of muffins was just delivered, and we have juices, water, coffee, tea?"

"No, thank you, I'm fine." She rubbed her hands together, then sat on them to conceal their trembling. "What's this about?"

"We understand that you accused someone of sexually assaulting you yesterday. Was the person in the dining room when you mentioned this?"

She shook her head, her whole body shaking now. "I don't want to talk about it."

"Did someone threaten you?"

She shook her head, all color drained from her already sallow cheeks.

"Jade, we can protect you. If there's someone here who frightens you, we'll have them confined?"

"It won't matter. The damage is done. Do you think I want to be like this?" she said, running her hands down the sides of her body. "I was fifteen. He destroyed my life."

"Can you tell us his name?"

"Cooper... Jerry Cooper. He wasn't on the retreat list, you see. I never would have come if I'd known he'd show up."

"Yes, well, rest assured, we'll make certain he's never in your presence again. I also intend to charge him if you're willing to testify."

"No. I can't."

"Can you tell us briefly how it happened?"

"He came to the house looking for our father. They're in the same department. English, at Greenleaf."

"Still are, I understand."

She nodded. "They went in his study. I was upstairs studying when our father called to me, asked me to go to the garage and fetch our old wagon as he had a number of boxes he was giving to him."

"What was in them, do you know?"

"Old files and things related to a course, I think. Anyway, since he'd walked, he had no way to get them home, so my father asked me to walk him home and bring the wagon back. He was kind of creepy, but also friendly, so I went. It was impossible to say no to Father.

"When we got to his house, we carried the boxes in, and he asked me if I wanted lemonade. It was a hot day, so I said yes. As I was drinking my lemonade, he started talking about how pretty I was. Then he began fiddling with my hair. I said I'd better get going, but as I stood up, he grabbed me and pulled me onto the sofa. He was much bigger than me, and much stronger."

Tears rolled down her cheeks as Jade paused, her face a mask of pain and horror. She swallowed, then continued. "He just pushed me down, pulled off my shorts and underpants, then did it. I tried to scream, but he put one hand over my mouth. At one point, I was afraid I'd suffocate. Then it was over.

"He grabbed my clothes and told me to get dressed. There was blood on the sofa. He noticed it and said, 'That wasn't so bad, was it?

Now you're a woman.' Then he told me I'd better hurry home or my dad would be worried. That was the day I died."

Demaris reached across and laid his hands on hers, which were now resting in her lap. "Jade, I am so sorry this happened to you. Have you ever sought help? A therapist or counselor?"

"No."

"Did you tell anyone?"

"Ashlyn, but not then. Not until recently, when we ran into him in town and I threw up in a trash barrel on Main Street. Our mom died when I was two. I don't remember her, and Ashlyn has only faint memories. Our father was very strict. He wouldn't have understood and would probably have blamed me for being flirtatious."

"Is that really true, do you think?"

She shrugged her bony little shoulders. "I don't know, but I was so shattered inside that I couldn't."

"He'll be punished," Demaris said, his seething anger at Cooper threatening to overwhelm him.

"What does it matter now?"

"It matters. Jade, I'd like to ask you one more question, then Detective Dugan, Pete, will escort you back. Is that okay?"

She nodded.

"Did you ever see Mr. Bailey around campus?"

"Once in a while. He only came in the summer. He was a dirty old lech, always sleeping with students. He even made a pass at Ashlyn one summer, but she set him straight. She's strong, not weak like me."

"You are far from weak, and none of Cooper's attack was your fault. You know that, don't you?"

She shrugged. "As I said, what does it matter?"

"And as I said, it matters. One more question about Mr. Bailey. Did you know any of the young women who succumbed to him?"

"No, but there were plenty who loved shagging profs for better grades, believe me."

"Thank you, Jade. I know this was difficult. Pete will walk you back and one of us or one the other officers will be watching over you until this situation is resolved."

"Okay," she replied in a weak, shaky voice.

As soon as the door closed behind them, Demaris grabbed his phone and called Greta, instructing her to find Cooper and have him confined to his room until further notice. "Assign a full-time guard and have his meals brought to him. Under no circumstances is he to venture anywhere else around the inn or grounds, understood?"

Then he sat at the table, head in hands, wondering if he should call Chief Smith and have Cooper locked up. Then he decided against it. Instead, he began making a list of whom he would visit in Greenleaf. *If I can't get Jade to testify, I can at least ensure that Dr. Cooper no longer has a job at the college. Even if it takes years, I will ruin him.*

CHAPTER 30

Fifteen minutes after calling Greta, Demaris strolled through the front parlor and grabbed Marilyn Lively as she was heading into breakfast alone, her husband nowhere to be seen. "Might I have a minute of your time, Ms. Lively?"

"Of course," she said, accompanying him to the now-empty west parlor, its Victorian furnishings now returned to their places after yoga. Chairs and sofas covered in faded blue velvet and chintz were arranged in conversational proximity, surrounded by walls papered in washed out brocade. The décor seemed oddly out of place with its ocean backdrop.

As they sat in stiff, uncomfortable chairs, their lacy antimacassars askew and wrinkled, he wondered why the Vickerses had neglected to update the otherwise beautiful space.

"How can I help you, Lieutenant?"

"I just have a few questions. One is about your relationship with Fawn Davis and Kyle Robles."

"We're friends and have been for years."

"Friends? Nothing more?"

She eyed him for a few seconds, then said, "I'm assuming you've heard gossip about Kyle and me?"

Surprised by this new information, he said. "Actually, it's your husband's activities I was interested in, specifically his activities when teaching summer courses at Greenleaf, but of course, should you wish to elaborate about your and Mr. Robles's relationship, please feel free."

She rolled her eyes in what seemed to be a forced and exaggerated attempt at nonchalance. "You must be referring to Beck's pathetic little dalliances? In those days, my husband and I had an open marriage, but only in the summer. He did his thing, and I did mine."

"And that worked for you?"

"We're still together, aren't we? Besides, monogamy is seriously overrated, don't you think?"

Ignoring her question, he said, "So while your husband was carrying on with Greenleaf coeds, you were home spending time with Mr. Robles? Where was Fawn in all this?"

"Open marriage? Do you understand the concept, dear?"

"So, Fawn also participated in this lifestyle?"

"Honey, Fawn invented it. She was the woman having babies out of wedlock left and right, then giving them away."

"Excuse me. Did you say babies?"

She shrugged. "That's always been the word on the street."

"And do you know how many and who the fathers were?"

"I only know about Jerry. We knew all about Daisy's origins way before she did. I mean, we didn't know Fawn and Kyle then, but we'd heard rumors after we got together."

"Mr. Robles is quite a bit younger than you, is he not?"

"Younger than Fawn too. I've dated several younger men over the years. I mean, if you're gonna sleep around on your boring hubby, you might as well go for younger and virile, or why bother?"

Why bother indeed, Demaris thought. "Well, I'll let you get to breakfast. Are you still going through with today's schedule?"

"Might as well since we're trapped here. Truth be told, Nancy and I would just as soon cancel the whole thing and head home. By the way, she knows nothing about what we've just been discussing, and

I'd like to keep it that way. She's a dear friend, but a recent one, who knows nothing about our swinging singles days."

Lucky her, he thought, but simply said, "We'll see what we can do."

As Lively sashayed from the room and across the parlor, he followed and found Stevens posted by the dining room door. "So, she went to breakfast?" he asked his junior officer.

"Yes, sir, and she's eating like a horse."

"Good. I hope she can keep it down."

CHAPTER 31

The usual table groupings formed at breakfast. Claire, Yorky, and Bob had almost finished when Jane and Bess sat down. "It's the yoga crowd," Bob said. "Gotta try that someday."

"Fawn's a fantastic instructor," Jane said.

As Georgia poured coffee and tea, Bess gazed around. She was surprised not to see Beck Bailey or the flamboyant Leo. The latter always made a grand entrance. "Georgia, have you seen Mr. Tallstory this morning?" she asked as the young woman filled her mug with tea.

"No, he wasn't at yoga, and we know how he likes to show off there. For an old guy, he's pretty limber."

Georgia was right—Leo did like to show off his flexibility. Bess smiled as she watched Georgia head off with their breakfast orders. Instead of the usual black slacks, Georgia wore yoga capris and her top, although white, was not crisp white cotton.

Reading her friend's thoughts, Jane said, "Anything goes at breakfast, I guess."

"How are you ladies holding up this morning?" Yorky asked, a smile reaching his kind eyes.

"Okay, and you

"I'll be glad to get home," he said.

Claire patted his arm. "I think we all will."

Bess nodded in agreement. "Have you seen Hillary, Ashlyn, and Jade?"

"They came, ate quickly and went for a walk, I think," Claire said. "There was a slight kerfuffle, then Jade ran out. The other two grabbed muffins and left just after her. Poor thing."

Before they could talk further, Angie appeared with their breakfasts. "Hey, everyone, Georgia had to run. I have two plates here. Who's having the johnnycakes?"

"I am," Bess said. "Thanks, Angie. Jane had eggs."

Jane looked up as Angie set her plate in front of her. "How are you? We didn't see you earlier."

"Bella sent me in to clean Mr. Cooper's room while he was with the police." She leaned down, voice low. "Apparently, he's now confined to his room for the day. What's that about, do you think?"

"First we've heard of it," Claire said, shaking her head. "I wonder why he ever came in the first place. Seems to rub everyone the wrong way."

Angie shrugged. "Seems nice enough to me, but then they never tell us anything."

"Where are you from?" Bob asked. "You look real familiar."

"Northport. That's where I grew up. My parents were killed in a car accident when I was little, and my grandma raised me. She lived in Northport."

"Does she still?" Jane asked.

Angie shook her head, her eyes registering sadness. "She passed away last year."

"Oh, I am sorry," Bess said. "Have you other family?"

"No... At least not that I know of. I was adopted. Someone left me on the steps of my parents' church, St. Mary of the Angels. My parents had to jump through a lot of hoops to adopt me."

Claire stared at her. "Did they ever trace your birth parents?"

She shook her head. "They tried, but then gave up. I was only a few days old, but none of the local hospitals had records of any births during that time."

"Didn't they try to look farther afield?" Claire asked, her face registering the shock they all felt.

Angie shrugged again. "My grandma didn't like to talk about it. I only found out when I went through her things after she died, then went to the priest at St. Mary's and social services. Their records sucked. Excuse me, I'm being summoned." She turned toward Bella Vickers, gesturing from the kitchen door, then turned back. "You know the weird thing? Of all the staff working here this summer, five of us are adopted. Strange, huh?"

Bess wanted to ask who the other adoptees were, but Angie hurried off.

"Strange indeed," Claire said. "You're right, Bob. She does look familiar, and now I know why. I'm in Northport constantly for this and that. I've probably seen her around town."

As they finished their breakfasts, Marilyn and Nancy stopped by the table to let them know the morning workshop would begin in twenty minutes. As they rose to head up to their rooms for folders and notes, Bess spied Angie clearing another table. "Let's ask her," she said, heading across the room.

"Ask her what?" Jane asked, trailing behind her friend.

Angie stopped her work and gazed up as they neared. "Can I get something for you ladies?"

"I was just wondering," Bess said. "Who are the other adoptees among you?"

"Well, there were five with Daisy, but now there's Georgia, Henry, Matt, and me. Weird, huh?"

"Thanks Angie. See you at lunchtime."

Bess didn't offer an opinion, but as they climbed the stairs to their rooms, Jane said, "Weird indeed. Everything around this place and this week is weird, but you better be careful. You were stepping over the 'no-sleuthing' line back there. Better hope your hubby doesn't find out."

"He won't. Besides, I'm sure they know all about the adoption thing. They would have uncovered that through the interviews and background checks. Brendan's a wiz at research, Greta too."

DURING MARILYN AND NANCY'S JOINT MORNING WORKSHOP, DEMARIS decided to reinterview Fawn and Ashlyn. Much to Pete's dismay, his boss kept Greta and assigned him to help Stevens keep watch at the inn to make sure Cooper stayed put and that Jade was safe. Greta caught Ashlyn on her way to the workshop and brought her to the cottage where her boss awaited.

The creak of the cottage's rickety screen door heralded her arrival. Demaris looked up from his notes. "Thank you for coming, Ashlyn. We won't keep you long. Shall we sit here at the table?" He gestured to a chair opposite him. "Would you like water or soda?"

"Water would be great." She took her seat as Greta went to the fridge.

He waited while she unscrewed the bottle cap and took a sip. The exact opposite of her sister, Ashlyn was robust and athletic, with dark blue eyes, straight shoulder-length sandy hair, and rosy cheeks. Dressed in denim capris and a white summer top, she looked the picture of health and vitality. "I want to ask you a little about your teens."

"Whatever for?"

"Jade has told us about the attack when she was fifteen."

She regarded him with sad eyes. "Yes, that. I lost my sister then, but until a year ago, I never knew why."

"What are your recollections of that time? Were you ever approached by Mr. Cooper or anyone else?"

"Not that I remember. I'm older than Jade, and by the time she was fifteen, I was dating George, my husband. He was all I could think about, I'm afraid. I should have paid more attention to my poor sister. Then, I went away to college in Boston. When George and I married and settled in Greenleaf, Jade asked to live with us."

"How long did she stay?"

"She's still there. We have a guest cottage behind our home, and she lives there. The house was George's house growing up. His parents are both gone, and they left it to him. It works out...with Jade,

I mean. George travels constantly for work, so she keeps me company. Helps with our writing collaborations too.”

“Your husband’s a journalist, is he not?”

She nodded, brushing back strands of hair from her forehead and tucking it behind her ears. “He was hired by the *Times* right out of college.”

“He’s very talented. I see his byline from time to time.”

She smiled, a lovely open smile, and Demaris was struck again by the contrast between her and her sad, tortured sister. “Thank you.”

“Well, we’ll let you get back. You write a series, I understand, so you must be eager to learn from Ms. Lively and Ms. Pratt.”

“Yes, thanks.” She stood and took up her water bottle.

“Detective Burke and I will walk over with you.”

He grabbed a notebook and locked the cottage door behind him.

CHAPTER 32

Demaris turned his face to the sun, closing his eyes for several minutes. Every minute they spent here was perilous to everyone, including his team and the wife he loved so deeply. He wished he were here on vacation with Bess, enjoying the charming inn with its wide porches and comfortable rockers, not investigating this tangled web of liaisons and the murder of poor Daisy Davis. She sounded like a spoiled brat, but she didn't deserve to die, especially in this beautiful place.

A door creaked open, then he heard footsteps. Opening his eyes, he spied Greta and Fawn Davis approaching. He smiled, beckoning Fawn to take one of the three rockers he'd arranged. Greta pulled hers back and settled down with pen and notebook.

"Thank you, Fawn. We won't take too much of your time. How are you holding up?"

She shrugged, meeting his eyes, hers calm and serene. She then turned her attention to arranging her flowery silk duster over her knees and crossing her long lovely legs under billowing black pants. Her thick blonde hair was woven in one long braid draped over her shoulder.

"No worries about pulling me from in there. I love Marilyn and Nancy, but the workshop was a bit boring. I only came down because

Kyle was fussing about leaving me alone in the suite. I don't write series and never plan to do so."

"I wanted to ask you a bit more about your past, specifically your pregnancies. There have been two babies, I believe?" He saw Greta's face register shock, while Fawn's remained placid.

"So, your relentless digging has uncovered more sordid details about my life as a slut."

"I'm trying to make connections, Fawn. I'm not judging, but this is a murder investigation conducted in this place where so many people have intertwined histories. We've covered your relationship with Jerry Cooper."

"A mistake, but he's been a good friend over the years. As I told you, I met him shortly after my *Eat, Play, Love* travels when I was teaching a summer yoga retreat at Greenleaf. I was on a high after rebuilding my life and Jerry was there. I stupidly became pregnant, went home to Providence, and taught yoga till I gave birth. I met Kyle when I was six months pregnant. He was wonderful in those days. He was with me at the birth and always treated Daisy as his own daughter."

Demaris sat up. "I believe there was another man and another baby before your liaison with Jerry, wasn't there?"

"A mistake. A horrible, horrible mistake. They're dear friends. I never should have gone there. I was adrift, you see. Alone. I had no man in my life, and she was traveling all the time. He was lonely, and so was I. We only live a block apart. It just kind of happened. No one knows about it, including him, and I'd like to keep it that way.

"I left town when I realized I was pregnant. I went to my sister's in Ohio. Talk about living hell with her boorish husband and three horrid kids. I told people I was in school there, but I basically hid out and took classes to become certified as a yoga instructor. For the last two months of my pregnancy, Lotus Blossom, the yoga center near my sister, let me move in. They have a retreat space, and I needed to be alone. I worked for them until the baby was gone. I tried to arrange for her adoption, but it fell through. The couple were lunatics. So, I came back east, made arrangements here, and then she was gone, five days after her birth. I haven't any idea what happened to her." As she concluded, a tear snaked down her cheek, the calm placid mask replaced by infinite sadness. "I've missed her every day of my life."

Even though he knew the identity of the baby's father, he also knew he had to ask. Before he could open his mouth, a bloodcurdling scream came from the window above them. "He's dead, he's dead!" a woman's voice cried. "Help! Help! Help!"

CHAPTER 33

Stevens met him in the front parlor. "Sir, they think it's Tallstory. No one's seen him all day. Pete's up there and told me to wait here for you."

"Okay. You and Greta stay down here. No one goes up the stairs or elevator." Demaris glanced at the workshop group now huddled at the dining room door. After spying Bess and Jane, he turned and took the stairs two at a time.

Ron Vickers stood at the door to Leo Tallstory's room, preventing anyone from entering. Several of the staff stood around Georgia Carney, who was slumped in a chair, sobbing. "Georgia found him when she came to clean the room," Ron said.

Stepping past the inn owner, he spied Tallstory splayed across the king-size brass bed. Like Daisy, his throat had been slashed, probably from behind by the position of the body. His striped pajamas and the bed's patchwork quilt were saturated with his blood, his shiny, black mule slippers lying helter-skelter on the rug. Tallstory had impressed him as a tidy person so the slippers seemed jarringly out of place.

He turned to Pete. "Anyone else been in here?"

"No one except the maid, Georgia, and Mr. Vickers. And whoever killed him, of course."

"Call Megan and get her here ASAP. I'll call Chief Smith to bring all his guys back, Wilbur too. I want every inch of this place searched. Whoever did this had to have left covered in blood."

"Maybe not," Pete said, leading him to the bathroom where one of the inn's robes and several bloody towels were thrown in the clawfoot tub. The robe's sleeve and front were red with blood. "It looks like he or she undressed, put on the robe to kill him, then came in, washed up, and got dressed again."

Demaris shook his head, noticing a breakfast tray with a half-eaten muffin and remnants of scrambled eggs and bacon, an over-turned coffee cup, its contents now a dark brown stain on the room's braided rug. "All while Tallstory was having his breakfast? How did they slip in unnoticed? Unless it was someone he knew."

The crime scene crew arrived in record time, and Megan and her assistant were on their way in as Demaris stepped out into the hall to talk with Ron. "Did you see anything at all?"

"No. I've been doing the morning grocery pickup with Georgie. Just got back."

Since no one was allowed to leave, all food and other supplies were delivered from the village by local handyman, Joe Pelton, every morning. Each day, the two men met Joe at the ferry dock to transfer all the goods from his skiff.

"Where are the two organizers, Marilyn, and the Pratt woman? They can spread the word for their people to stay together, inside, in the dining room or parlor. I'd like to speak with everyone in a few minutes, including the staff, if you could gather them up.

"Sure thing."

Demaris turned back to the crime scene. As Vickers headed down the stairs, Marilyn Lively's voice reached them. "Where is he? The one in charge? I must speak to Lieutenant Demaris now!"

Moving toward the stairs he called, "I'm here, Ms. Lively."

Reaching the second floor, she ran forward, her appearance disheveled. Face red, eyes puffy, she appeared to have been crying. "He's gone! My Beck! We can't find him anywhere! I'm sick to death with worry! Please you've got to find him!"

He placed a hand on her shoulder, indicating a chair near the elevator. "When did you last see him?"

"I don't want to sit! You...we, we've got to find him, now!"

As Marilyn collapsed, sobbing, he gave her his handkerchief. "Was he at your workshop?"

"No, he said he had a headache and was going to take a walk to clear his head. Besides, he's heard our workshop, or variations of it, dozens of times."

"Did he go alone?"

"Of course, he did. Everyone else came to the workshop, except poor Leo, of course." She dabbed her eyes, his handkerchief now stained with mascara, her pale cheeks streaked with thick pancake makeup.

"I've got officers coming from Mattapoisett and the village. They'll scour the island. We'll find him."

She nodded. "But what can I do? I can't just sit around chatting about the writing process when my darling husband is missing."

"I'd like to join my men now. If you're up to it, I'd like you and Ms. Pratt to gather all your writers in the parlor. After lunch we'll know more, and I'll want to speak with everyone. I can ask Nancy to do it if that would be easier?"

"No, I'll find Nancy and we'll get right on it. You'll let me know when you find him? That is, when you have my Beck safe and sound?"

"Of course."

They descended to the first floor together, and Marilyn hurried toward the west parlor to find her codirector. Demaris motioned to Pete and Brendan and headed for the front door to greet the officers streaming out of cruisers on the lawn and driveway.

Bess and Jane intercepted him. Bess touched his arm, her lovely eyes full of concern. "What's happened?"

"Leo Tallstory has been killed and Beck Bailey is missing. Have either of you seen Bailey since breakfast?"

They both shook their heads.

"I've got to get the teams organized outside. Do not leave each other alone for a second. Tell that to all your fellow writers, please. No one should go or be anywhere alone. Ms. Lively's organizing a meeting at one. I'll come talk to everyone after lunch, okay?"

"I doubt anyone will feel like eating," Jane said.

"No, I expect not, but you'll be together, at least." He reached over and squeezed Bess's hand. "Take care, please." She nodded, and they watched him switch into cop mode, shoulders set as Pete pushed the front doors open and joined Greta on the porch.

He dispatched teams of two officers to various locations: the inn, barn and studio, smaller outbuildings, cliff path and the fields and woods around them. "What are you thinking, boss?" Pete asked as the two men started down the cliff path.

"I'm thinking that whoever murdered Daisy Davis killed Tallstory as well. I'm not sure what their connection was, but it all goes back to Fawn Davis and her indiscriminate sex life."

Pete shook his head. "She seems like a smart person. How did she not know about birth control?"

Demaris gave his second-in-command an eye roll, then scanned the area. Officers were visible everywhere, dotting the fields and wide-open property. Chief Smith had called down and had two boats launched to patrol the shoreline. "If we don't find him soon, I'll request the helo."

When RHD needed the services of a state police helicopter, one could be summoned to arrive in fifteen to twenty minutes. He prayed their services wouldn't be needed. As they continued on the cliff path, Pete pointed north where Stevens and an Old Harbor officer were struggling to open the door of a small, dilapidated shed. "What's that, do you think?"

"Looks like an old pump house. Don't remember seeing that before."

As they watched, the two officers wrenched the door open and disappeared inside. Stevens reappeared almost immediately, scanning his surroundings until he spotted the two men. "Hey, boss, Pete, we found him!"

As Demaris and Pete raced toward the others, he thought, *That's the first time Brendan's called me boss and not sir. Progress.*

When they reached the pump house, Stevens and Officer Rego from Old Harbor each had an arm and were dragging an unconscious but breathing Beck Bailey out. They hauled him a short distance to an open spot in the grass with help from Demaris and Pete. "Looks like he might've been knocked out," Brendan said. "He's got a bump on the back of his head."

"Pete, call for an ambulance. Now!"

After making the call, Dugan came to stand beside his boss. "They're on their way."

"Good."

Pete frowned. "So, he comes out here and someone whacks him on the head? Doesn't make sense. Why would he come out here anyway?"

"His wife said he wanted to take a walk after breakfast," Demaris said, bending over. "Mr. Bailey? Can you hear me?" He gently slapped his cheeks, careful not to shake him or move his neck.

Suddenly, there was a whooshing sound as the decrepit structure burst into flames. "What the hell?" Pete cried as they stepped back, dragging Bailey with them.

"Call Greta and have her get the fire department out here, now!" Demaris shouted to Pete, as they watched flames shoot into the sky. "Brendan, what did you find in there?"

"Not much, sir. Mr. Bailey was duct-taped to a big pipe, not very tightly. Billy cut him out easily. There was the old pump, papers and junk on the floor, and a battery-powered space heater. It looked weird 'cause it was the only new-looking thing in the place. I remember thinking I should go back and turn it off with all the old papers sitting around it."

"She rigged it," Bailey muttered as he tried to sit up. "She rigged it, then knocked me out.

"Whoa, Mr. Bailey," Demaris said. "Be careful. You've had a nasty knock on the head."

Brendan removed his jacket, rolled it, and put it under Bailey's head.

Demaris knelt beside Bailey. "What did you mean? Rigged it?"

"She crumpled a bunch of papers and arranged them around the heater just out of my reach."

"She?"

"It's that skinny one. Claims I'm her father. She's gone after Fawn. You better find them quick. Kid may be skinny, but she's strong as an ox."

"Mr. Bailey, who are you talking about?" Demaris asked, although he knew the name already.

"Geez, my head feels like crap." Bailey's eyes fluttered, and he passed out.

"Shit," Demaris said. "Call Greta. Tell her to find Fawn. Tell her not to let her out of her sight."

"Brendan, I need you and Officer Rego to stay here with Mr. Bailey until the ambulance arrives. We'll direct them to your location."

Rego appeared from the side of the burning pump house. "There's an old wheelbarrow back here, sir. Want us to wheel him back to the inn? Easier for the EMTs."

"No, I don't want to move him, just in case."

Stevens glanced at the young officer. The two had graduated from the academy together and started with the Old Harbor police the same year. Then he turned to Demaris. "No worries, sir. We'll take care of him."

"Thanks, Brendan. Go with them in the ambulance. If they give you any trouble about it, call me. Comprende?"

"Yes, sir."

"Let's go," he said, nudging Pete. "I pray we aren't too late."

CHAPTER 34

As they neared the inn, they spied Greta standing over Fawn Davis, who was seated in one of the rockers. Most of the writers group stood around them. The minute Demaris laid eyes on her, he knew.

"That's why her daughter's always looked so familiar," he said.

Pete gazed over at him. "What daughter?"

"Where is she?" he called to Greta, then Fawn.

Greta waved her arms. "They're searching now, boss. Officers are everywhere."

Hands on hips, Pete looked back and forth between his boss and Greta. "What daughter? What's going on?"

"Come on," Demaris said, patting his shoulder. "We'll take the back of the inn, ocean side. I'll explain on the way."

Fawn sprang from her seat. "I'm coming with you!"

"No!" he called as they started running. "Greta, keep the others here!"

As they rounded the building, there was no time to explain when they spied her standing on a granite outcropping at the cliff's edge.

~

At first glance, she seemed small and waif-like, but there was also a resilience and strength in her stance, that inner core of power that had carried her over the years. Carried her to this place where she had confronted her half sister, the daughter her mother had kept. The daughter she'd loved and nurtured, unlike the earlier one, discarded like a piece of trash on the steps of St. Mary of the Angels. It had been easy to slit Daisy's throat, the spoiled brat.

She turned, gazing eastward over their heads at the smoke accompanied by the wailing of the fire engines. "Looks like my deadbeat father is dead, she muttered. "Good riddance. What a spineless jellyfish. When I told him about me, he sputtered about how he hadn't known. Pathetic! I'm sorry about clueless Leo. He might have been pompous, but he was always kind to me, listening when I told about my poems, and my dull, pitiful existence."

Demaris slowed to a walk, not wanting to frighten her. "Angie, come down, please! We can help you."

"Yeah, right. Help me to prison for life. No, thanks."

From behind, Demaris heard the others and then Fawn. "No, baby, please! It's all my fault."

Angie turned her tearstained face to confront her mother. "Don't you dare! Don't you dare call me baby! You have no right to call me that. Ever!"

Fawn came to stand beside him. "I know... I know I don't. But Angie, please... I'm so sorry...so sorry."

"Get out of my sight, you bitch!"

"Fawn, it may not be helping to have you here," he said quietly.

She stood beside him, glazed eyes staring up at her daughter. "She looks so much like Daisy."

"Shut up! Do what he says and go away."

Tears in her eyes, Fawn nodded and turned toward the inn. She walked slowly, climbed to the porch, and disappeared through the back door. Not once did she look back. As the door closed, Angie lost her footing for an instant and threw her arms out to steady herself.

"Angie, come on. You've got your whole life ahead of you. You've got your father and mother and—"

"Don't call them that! Those people are not my parents!"

"You seem to have gone to a lot of trouble to establish that they are." Taking small steps, he had managed to get less than ten feet from the outcropping.

"Did you see her? She never even looked back, just like the day she left me on those church steps. The people who rescued me? Those were my parents, and they're gone. I did what I did because the people who conceived me deserved to be punished. They were both selfish, rich kids who threw their helpless infant away, at least in her case. He was so busy screwing around, he claims he didn't even know I existed. Bullshit, of course. When I put a knife to his fat, jowly throat, he admitted that she told him back then that she was pregnant and that it was his. What did he do? Nothing. Offered to pay for an abortion."

Less than five feet from the base of the rock now, Demaris calculated the likelihood of catching her should she jump. Her tiny face streaked with tears, Angie was trembling, white shirt spotted with red, pants torn. *Like a child fallen from her bicycle*, he mused, shuffling to the side and forward.

She raised her hand. "Stay back. Your lackey too. Don't think I don't see what you're doing. Trying to box me in."

"Angie, it must be cold for you up there. Let us get you down. Get you a blanket."

"What are you, nuts? The second I get off this rock, the only thing you'll get me is handcuffs and a trip to jail."

It's true, of course, he thought sadly. They'd find a blanket, but she was going first to the cells in Mattapoisett, then MCI in Framingham. "I want to hear your story, and then we can determine what's best."

"What's best is for me to go. Tell your wife goodbye. She's a nice lady." With that, Angela Smith, heartbroken and alone, turned toward the ocean and dove headfirst off the cliff, plunging to the rocks below.

"Shit," he yelled, scaling the rocks as Pete circled and began climbing down the steep embankment. When he reached where she'd stood, Demaris looked down at the tiny form below, lying broken on the rocks, her arms and legs splayed at unnatural angles. As he watched, Pete reached her, checked her pulse, and looked up, shaking his head.

Tears clouded his eyes as Demaris heard a scream from the inn. He turned to see Fawn burst out the door. "No, no, no!" Behind her, Greta appeared, attempting to hold her back as the others gathered on the porch.

"Everyone stay back!" he yelled. "It's over."

He retrieved his phone and called for an ambulance, then searched the crowd for Bess. Their eyes met, and he knew he was home. *Safe.*

EPILOGUE

Nancy Pratt called the editors and agents scheduled to come the following day. She promised the retreat participants that they would reschedule these as Zoom meetings in the weeks to come. After brief follow-up statements, everyone was cleared to leave for home. All except for Jerry Cooper, whom Demaris intended to charge as soon as they could investigate more fully. They held him in Mattapoisett overnight, then released him, but Demaris felt sure that Cooper had left a trail of victims, and he intended to find them.

Ron and Bella closed the inn for a month and took Clara to Key West, a long-postponed vacation. Fawn returned to Providence with Kyle as her protector. Demaris gave that arrangement two months. Marilyn kept her head held high and went home with Beck. Wilma and Bob Franklin happily returned to Old Harbor, she to her cats and Bob to his daughter Rosemary and his boats.

One happy outcome of the gathering at Gooseberry was the warm relationship that had developed between Claire Rubin and Yorky Strauss. As they said their goodbyes, she had leaned over to Demaris, smiling as she whispered, "We're talking about moving in together. Am I crazy?"

He returned her smile, happy for them. Claire had endured such an abusive second marriage to a pompous, cruel philanderer. She deserved happiness. "Not at all. I wish you all the best. He seems like a great guy."

A week later, Bess and Roger invited the team for dinner, a gathering that included Jane and Hillary. Scents of saffron and spices filled the house as they chatted over Bess's cioppino, a crisp field greens salad, and crusty bread.

"Bess, this is amazing!" Hillary said, dipping her bread into the spicy red broth swimming with fish, lobster, littlenecks, and scallops. "I would love the recipe."

Bess smiled. "Of course. I'm guessing you can find a wonderful recipe online, but I'll write it down for you."

Roger gazed over at his wife, his eyes warm. Her cheeks were aglow, her eyes sparkled, and he thought he'd never seen her looking so lovely. Of course, he had the same thought every time she walked into a room. Watching her, he was reminded of Rumi's poem, "The Most Alive Moment."

"So, not to spoil the evening," Jane said, "but did Angie's service go okay?"

"Poor kid. It was rough," Roger said, remembering how he and Pete had stood with tiny group circling the grave, Fawn sobbing, held upright by Kyle Robles. Beck Bailey beside them. Marilyn had been nowhere in sight.

Jane set down her spoon and gazed at him. "How did she find out about Fawn and Beck?"

"Through her adoptive mother's papers. When Angie went through her grandmother's desk after her death last year, she discovered that her parents had hired a detective years ago to learn her birth parents' identity in case they ever needed to contact them for health reasons. Martha Smith was very religious and wanted to know the identity of the monster who had abandoned her precious daughter on the church steps. The detective not only found Fawn, but Beck Bailey as well."

"How did she get Beck to the pump house?" Bess asked. By tacit agreement, she and Roger had avoided discussing the case until now as she could see it had unsettled him greatly.

Greta set down her fork. "Bailey was out walking, and Angie waylaid him, not for the first time. She started talking again about him being her father. He waved her off, telling her she was crazy, and she hit him with a rock. Knocked him out and dragged him to the pump house. For a little person, she was strong."

"And she had the wheelbarrow," Brendan said.

Jane gazed over at Roger. "Why did Tallstory have to die? He didn't have any connection to Angie, did he?"

"Leo overheard a heated conversation between Angie and Bailey the day before, when she first confronted him," Greta said.

Bess stared at her husband. "You mean Beck and Leo knew the day before and never said anything to anyone?"

Roger shrugged. "I have a hunch that Tallstory may not have known what the conversation was about, but Angie couldn't have known that for sure. Bailey may have told Marilyn. Claims he didn't, and she concurred."

Pete nodded. "Yeah, she pretended she knew nothing when we questioned her, but her hysterics when he went missing seemed a little over the top."

"How's Fawn holding up?" Jane asked, knowing from Bess that Roger had visited her the day before.

"Shattered, but she's a strong woman. I predict she'll pull through with or without Robles or Cooper, the latter of whom I intend to throw in jail for what he did to Jade Temple."

Hillary sighed. "Poor Jade. She's such a sweetheart...if she could just get healthy. Ashlyn and her husband have persuaded her to go into a treatment center."

"Good," Roger said. "Now let's put Gooseberry Island behind us for the rest of the evening, shall we? As some of Bess's and my favorite people, I'm grateful beyond words that you're all safe, and it's time for dessert. I hope you like floating island?"

❧

LATER, AFTER THEIR GUESTS DEPARTED, BESS AND ROGER CLEARED THE table and washed up, chatting about their plans for his kids' upcoming visit. Bess had embraced Teresa and Owen as her own and had lovingly furnished and decorated their rooms. Their visits from Ohio were always a high point for the couple, especially poignant for Roger, who had only recently learned of Owen's existence.

As it was a warm evening, they decided to have tea on the back porch and settled into comfortable Adirondack chairs, adjacent, their hands touching one another's. As they looked out over fields and wildflowers and the sea beyond, Roger reached over and squeezed her hand. "I love you," he said, stroking her soft skin, their fingers linking.

"I love you too. It's so good to be home."

"Yes."

❧

Please read for sample chapters of the first Ricky Steele mystery, *Prepped to Kill.*

PREPPED TO KILL

Chapter 1

Wednesday, the turning point. My weeks begin with such promise—dreams of selling a novel or short story, fantasies of the *Globe* calling to offer me a regular column, hopes of breaking two hundred in tips in one night of waitressing or getting a call for a huge glass commission. Tuesday, the dream is fading. By Wednesday, reality settles in, it's a week like all the others—too many odd jobs, too little money and too many bills cascading through the mail slot. At a time when many people my age—fifty-eight—were retiring, I was still living from paycheck to paycheck, job to job. Retirement for me would be keeling over in the middle of a project without so much as a "bye, bye life."

The phone's ring sucked me from the bog of self-pity. I considered not answering. No doubt it was a collection agency. I'm on a first name basis with several of their agents. On the fifth ring, curiosity won out. "Ricky Steele."

"Dorothy, is that you, dear?"

No one calls me Dorothy, at least no one expecting a response, and they certainly don't follow it with "dear." The voice was eerily familiar.

"This is Ricky."

"This is Muriel Petty, dear."

Muriel Petty, Muriel Petty... I knew the name and the association was not pleasant. A crazed dentist? The fascist kennel owner who lectures me about my cat's flea infestations prior to charging me two nights' tips to exterminate them.

"Your headmistress, dear, from Miss Whitley's?"

"Oh, yes, Mrs. Petty, what a surprise." Any more surprised and I'd have swallowed my tongue. Sixteen again, I bowed in her presence, feeling her beady eyes boring into me as she harangued me concerning some harmless prank. Muriel never saw my tears, her continual threats of expulsion bouncing off me like ping-pong balls. I longed to be expelled and she knew it.

"How are you, Dorothy?" The sickeningly sweet voice, its cadences usually followed by a lightning bolt of reprobation.

Only five days into my stay at Miss Whitley's School for Girls, Muriel had summoned me to her office and demanded that I "shape up." She was not about to let "one wayward, motherless girl incite the other girls to disobedience."

What could the old bat want? Hadn't I read a few years or decades ago that she'd retired? She must be about two hundred by now.

"Dorothy? Are you still there? I asked how you are, dear."

I shook myself. Could I be hallucinating after too much junk food and not enough sleep? "Fine," I croaked.

"Reunion Weekend is coming up. Are we going to see you?"

Not unless I'm bound and gagged and dragged there in a drunken stupor. "Gee, I hadn't planned on it."

"Oh, I was hoping. It being your fortieth and all."

"Well, I've kind of lost touch."

"Let me be frank, dear. I have another reason for calling."

"Oh?" That was a big surprise.

"I'd like to hire you."

Did they need a waitress? Was there some last minute touch-up painting needed in the Green Room? Did they need a snappy paragraph or two for the reunion brochure? And why in the world would she think of me? As a major Whitley donor, my father often attended reunion functions, but somehow, I couldn't imagine him recommending the services of his estranged daughter.

"For what?"

"We need a private investigator. Someone who knows the school and will be discreet."

Me, a private investigator? Now I knew I was hallucinating. Then, with sickening clarity, I remembered my teeny, tiny practical joke at Whitley School's expense—the notes for the alumni bulletin. Several months ago, having just finished reading the latest Sara Paretsky, I had assumed the role of V.I. Warshawski, or was it Sue Grafton and Kinsey Millhone? Whatever my wicked, perverse mood and persona, I had gleefully filled in my "class news card," describing my life as a PI. It was all a big yuk, to give our class agent, Bitsy Wedgehammer, a little laugh. And, Bitsy, the ditz, must've printed it.

I rifled through months of mail in a basket by the phone and extracted the *Whitley Wheel*. There it was in the "Class of 1968 News," one of only three entries. "Dorothy Steele writes from Fall River, Mass. that her private investigating company is thriving. The intrepid sleuth takes only the most difficult cases involving murder and mayhem, so watch out bad guys!"

"But, Mrs. Petty," I sputtered, picturing my hands tightening round Bitsy's scrawny little neck. "It was a joke."

"I can assure you, my dear, this is no joke."

Uh-oh, she's pissed. I remembered a time freshman year when we'd leaned out our third-floor dorm window and sprinkled talcum powder—our idea of a snowstorm in September—on Muriel's best coat as she swished through the front portico to attend a Board meeting. Spider Man in high gear couldn't have taken the stairs faster than Muriel.

"No, Mrs. Petty, not you. You see, I assumed Bitsy, Elizabeth, would catch my entry and edit it out. I never expected. Well, I just didn't think. Oh, I am sorry."

"Oh, don't be silly, dear. I haven't time."

What was I, fifty-eight or fifteen? Hadn't I just explained away this misunderstanding? "I'm not being silly. It's just—"

"We want to hire you, dear. I understand from your father that you're between jobs."

So, Dad had gotten into the act, although I could not imagine him lying on my behalf, especially about my being a private eye.

"He's speaking at Saturday's Luncheon, you know."

"You mean to tell me that my father recommended me for this job?"

"Oh, heavens no. But when we chatted a few months ago he told me you were looking for work. Is that wise at your age, not to have a steady income? Then, when I read about you in the *Wheel*, I put two and two together and thought you'd be perfect for our little problem. And, Dorothy, dear, we are counting on your discretion. Please keep this conversation private, even from your dear father. No one knows about any of this except myself and Dinny, I mean Donald, Mr. Petty, our current Head."

Dinny, now there was a blast from the past. The name conjured up adolescent fantasies about the tall, handsome English teacher, fresh out of college, with whom we'd all been madly in love. Ah, Dinny—the ideal of male perfection, his only flaw his unfortunate connection to Aunt Muriel.

"What am I supposed to be discreet about?"

"We've had some unpleasantness. I'll fill you in when you get here."

"I'm sorry, Mrs. Petty. I don't think I'm the woman for this job. What about a local person? Isn't there someone up there in Westfield who could—"

"Oh, good heavens, no! For obvious reasons, we don't want to use anyone from the community."

"What're we talking about here?"

"Does this mean you'll take the job?"

"No."

"Then I'd rather not say. Too bad, though. When a donor offered to pay a ten-thousand-dollar retainer for a week's work, I thought you'd jump at the chance, you being out of work and all."

"Ten thousand dollars?" I could feel her smirk.

"That's right. Please reconsider, Dorothy. Whitley needs you."

"Well, I…"

"We just want you to take a quiet look around. Help us put a stop to some shenanigans."

"Like?"

"Some minor acts of vandalism, a few thefts, some nasty mail, that sort of thing. And then this morning, we've had a student run off."

"Have you phoned the police?"

"Not yet. We can't have a swarm of police milling around during Reunion Weekend. Why, we've just gotten rid of them after the unpleasantness last week."

"Oh? And what was that?"

"A very sad business, really. One of our teachers took her own life. She was extremely popular, so it's been very hard on the students. We've had counselors on campus all week. We don't need another upset right now. Besides, Missy Franklin's a bit of a wild child. Not unlike yourself at that age. No doubt she's run off to spite her parents. As I recall, you made a few escapes yourself."

Was the woman actually trying to be chummy, making light of my many acts of rebellion and insubordination? Giving my head a shake, I pushed the reasons behind my many escapes to the far recesses of my mind. "This really does sound like something the police should be handling."

"Just a week. That's all we ask. Come to the reunion, enjoy your chums, and take a look around. You always were a devious girl. I should think you'd jump at the chance."

Stifling a flippant remark, my brain chanting its new mantra—"ten thousand dollars"—I said, "Sure, why not?"

"Delightful! When can you be here?"

"Tomorrow afternoon?"

"Oh, Dorothy, you are a lifesaver. I'll call Dinny right now. He'll be delighted."

We made arrangements for me to call when I got into Westfield and I rang off. "Dinny," I murmured, wondering if I could diet away twenty pounds in twenty-four hours.

Muriel Petty enlisting my help? Stranger things have probably happened, but certainly not to me.

Chapter 2

Half an hour later, I came to my senses and dialed information for Westfield, Massachusetts. As the phone rang, I flipped through the assortment of junk mail and stack of bills heralding my descent into debtors' hell. The recorded message came on asking "what city, what listing?" and I hung up. I had no choice. I would have to play private eye. I've read hundreds of mysteries. I know how V.I. does it. I know how Spencer does it. How hard could it be to pretend for one week?

Instead of calling Muriel Petty, I phoned Bunny Stark, my childhood friend, travel agent and realtor extraordinaire. She answered on the first ring with a cheery, "Stark and Company, Bunny speaking."

"Hey, Bun."

"Ricky, where you been, girl? I've been tryin' to get you all week. Wanna meet me at the G.C. for dinner tomorrow? Gotta use up the monthly assessment."

"You know I hate the Club. Take one of your clients and let's you and I go to the Rainbow. In fact, I was thinking of dragging Vinnie there tonight. Wanna meet us? Chorizo rolls dripping with grease?"

"Yuck, Ricky—think of your arteries. We're not getting any younger, you know."

"So, do you wanna join us? We'll start the healthy living program tomorrow."

"No can do. Got a date."

"With Mr. Wonderful?"

"No, Chad the Charmer flew the coop two weeks ago. This is a client, Devon Greenlaw, just moved into town. I helped him find a rental and he's taking me to dinner as a thank-you."

"And?"

"He's pretty cute, but who knows. After Chad, I'm ready for a breather. What 'bout you? Seeing anyone?"

"Not unless you count Vinnie and Cal, the plumber. Cal and I have become bosom buddies since my cesspool backed up."

"You should put in a septic system. Really helps with resale. Want me to see if Devon has a friend?"

Just what I needed. Devon was probably fifteen—Bunny likes 'em young—and his friend covered with peach fuzz and acne. "Thanks, Bun, maybe another time." I filled her in about my Whitley trip.

After telling me I was crazy and a host of other unflattering things, she agreed to look into accommodations in the Westfield area and get back to me. Next, I rang my neighbor, Vinnie Silvia, leaving a message on his machine about dinner. Then, I called the Lizzie's, the restaurant where I work in Fall River. It's named for Lizzie Borden, the alleged ax murderess, one of the city's major claims to fame. My boss, Leo, was none too happy to hear I needed a week off, but what could he say? It wasn't like he had to pay me while I was gone and, since I'm "one of his most reliable girls," he has to be nice to me.

Having frittered away a good chunk of the day, I got down to work. I have a number of part-time jobs—waitressing, house painting, writing short pieces for the local rag, and stained glass work. The latter two occupied the rest of my day. I had five book reviews to finish for the *Grove Gazette*, and two leaded glass window repairs for the Catholic Church.

It was unusual for the Catholic Church to hire me. I've done lots of work for the Protestants and Episcopalians, but the Catholics take their leaded glass seriously and usually contract out to the big firms in Boston. These two small panels were probably a test. I hate repairs—they're a pain in the butt—but I needed the money, so I knuckled down and completed the work.

Vinnie called at five thirty saying he would stop by in an hour. "Dinner's on me, Rick, no bullshitting." No argument here. After cleaning up, I set the two panels inside the garage door, ready for the church sexton to pick up in the morning. Then I faxed my reviews to the *Gazette* and showered. As I stood at my open closet, contemplating my private eye wardrobe, Vinnie knocked at the front door.

"Rick, you back there?" Vinnie's voice is like rich, deep velvet, one notch above a growl. If I was curvier, sexier, younger, and crazier, I'd be trying to lure him into my bed. As it was, I had watched too many women—girls, let's be honest—parade in and out of his house to ever hitch my wagon to his smoldering star. Vinnie is in his late fifties, same as me, but he looks thirty with the body of a mini Arnold Schwarzenegger in his heyday. Working out is a religion for Vinnie and he spends three or four hours of every day at the local gym. He says that gym time is business, and I don't ask questions.

Grabbing my sweatshirt and patting Beaky, my miniature tabby cat, I ran out, joining Vinnie for the short walk to the Rainbow. Vinnie and I live in Ocean Grove, a tiny beachfront community of ricky-ticky beachfront houses with postage stamp yards. I met Vinnie the day I moved into the "fixer-upper" Bunny sold me for "such a deal." With Vinnie's help I reroofed, painted and reshingled the entire house. Without his help, I'd still be up on the roof trying not to fall off or swallow a mouthful of roofing nails.

Along with every other woman in the place, I watched Vinnie's catlike sidle from bar to table. My height, Vinnie is twice as wide, his long, dark hair brushed back. It's the kind of thick, wavy hair women love to run their fingers through, before moving on to other parts of his anatomy. His coal-black bedroom eyes sparkled with mischief as he winked at a blonde at the next table. Sliding in beside me, he plunked two Buzzards Bay drafts in front of me. "What's up?"

"Not much. How 'bout you?" I moved my chair to block his view of the blonde.

He laughed, leaning back in his chair. "Rick, you kill me." With a final wink to Blondie, he leaned forward, directing his attention my way. "How's the love life? You still screwin' around with that online shit?"

"None of your business."

"No luck, I'm guessin.' Want me to set you up? I know a couple of guys."

"Who will not be my type."

"More your type than that last loser, what was his name?"

"Richard." My hand shot up. "Let's not talk about Richard, okay?"

"Well, first off, he was about a hundred."

"Sixty-eight. And that's talking about him."

"That's twenty years too old for you, Rick. You need a young guy. Somebody fun, who'll treat you right. Not some old crotchety drunk who's cryin' in his beer for his dead wife."

"It was martinis, thank you, and I think we've said enough about Richard."

"Not to mention that other twit. Kevin, wasn't it? What a self-absorbed little prick. What'd you ever see in him, anyway?"

"Who knows?" How had we gotten on this depressing subject? It couldn't all be the men's fault. Truth was, I wasn't very good at relationships.

"You ever see the little perv nowadays?"

"He wasn't a perv."

"Okay, how about a close-minded, lying, cheating little bigot?"

"Vinnie—enough!"

"So, am I wrong? What did I say that wasn't true?"

"Nothing, except for the perv part."

"So, is he still harassing you?"

"No. I run into his sister sometimes. Apparently, he's dating a twenty-year-old massage therapist."

"Exactly."

I decided not to ask what he meant by "exactly." "New subject. What's next week like for you? You here or on the road?"

"I'll be around. What'dya need?"

"Beaky needs you. I have to go away." I gave him a brief rundown of my plans.

"You, a private eye? Wait'll I tell the guys at the gym. They love hearin' about all the crazy shit you get into, but this tops everything. Gotta hand it to you, babe."

Nobody except Vinnie gets to call me "babe." "It is pretty ballsy, isn't it?"

"Ballsy and dangerous."

"I've survived divorce, breast cancer, and a bunch of other crap the past five years. I think I can handle this."

Vinnie's gaze softened. My husband's desertion predated our friendship, but he'd been through two mastectomies with me, bringing me hot soup and pasta, accompanying me on painfully slow walks, nary a flinch at the drains dangling below my sweatshirt like four turkey basters. "What if the suicide turns out to be murder?"

"At Whitley School? No way."

"What? Murderers can't get past the gates of Snotty High?"

"It's not that. It's just, well, the woman died in her car, in her garage. Of carbon monoxide poisoning. That's classic suicide."

"Maybe, maybe not. Be careful, Rick, that's all I'm saying."

Al set a steaming plate of chorizo rolls in front of us and we dove at them, savoring every mouthful of spicy sausage, fat soaking through spongy rolls, the whole crusty mess a deep, warm orange.

An hour later we strolled home, arm in arm, stuffed with greasy food and slightly buzzed after one too many drafts. If I were a wayward girl, I'd have invited Vinnie back to my place, but I value him too much as a friend. Besides, he's not my type. Much too nice.

Get *Prepped to Kill!*

ACKNOWLEDGMENTS

Thank you to my friend and neighbor, Sgt. Jason Pacheco of the Fall River, Massachusetts Police Department, for talking with me about police procedures. Any missteps in this area are entirely mine as he is always clear and professional. I am indebted to Dona Burke for her pioneering work and good humor as we grappled together to learn book formatting and for the *extraordinary wizardry* of the Formatting Fairies in continuing the process! No one could ask for a more perceptive, talented cover designer than Ashley Lopez. She gets it absolutely right every time! Most importantly, I would like to thank my dear family and friends, who are always there, no matter where life's travels take me. They make every day a miracle.

ALSO BY M. LEE PRESCOTT

Contemporary romances and mysteries by M. Lee Prescott include:

The Ricky Steele Mysteries

Prepped to Kill

Gadfly

Lost in Spindle City

Poof

Lady Love: A Cautionary Tale

Also, featuring Ricky Steele

Jigsaw

Roger and Bess Mysteries

A Friend of Silence

In the Name of Silence

The Silence of Memory

Silencing the Pen

Contemporary Romances

Well-Loved Romances

Widow's Island

Hestor's Way

Morgan's Run Romances

Emma's Dream

Lang's Return

Jeb's Promise

Rose's Choice

Hope's Wonder

Ruthie's Love

Polly's Heart

Kyle's Journey

Gus's Home

A Valley Christmas

Aria's Song

Bella's Touch

Mia's Crossing

Morgan's Fire Romances

Lucy's Hearth

Tim's Hands

Pam's Garden

Rich's Dilemma

Lolly's Wish

Greta's Goat

A Horseshoe Crab Cove Christmas

Joe's Calling

Young Adult Historical Romance

Song of the Spirit

A NOTE FROM THE AUTHOR

Thank you so much for taking the time to read *Silencing the Pen.* This is my fourth mystery featuring Bess Demaris and Roger Demaris and I am hoping to write many more in the years ahead.

If you liked **Silencing the Pen** and would be willing to write an review, I would be very grateful. Also, if you would like to hear my latest news, have access to bonus content, and receive notice of future book releases, please visit my website at *www.mleeprescott.com* and sign up for my newsletter. I promise I will not share your address, nor will I flood you with emails. Finally, this book has been revised, proofed and edited many, many times, but I, and my intrepid assistants, are human so if you spot a typo, please email me at *mleeprescott@gmail.com* and I will fix it.

Warm wishes,
M. Lee

Ways to Keep in touch:

Follow me on BookBub
https://www.bookbub.com/search/authors?search=M.+Lee+Prescott

Visit my website.
http://www.mleeprescott.com/

Check out my GoodReads pages
http://www.goodreads.com/author/show/7334813.M_Lee_Prescott

Follow me on Instagram *https://www.instagram.com/mleeprescottwriter/*
and Facebook *https://www.facebook.com/pages/M-Lee-Prescott/883010881714516*

and TikTok too.
https://www.tiktok.com/@mleeprescottwriter

ABOUT THE AUTHOR

M. Lee Prescott is the author of dozens works of fiction for adults, young adults, and children, among them **the Ricky Steele, Jigsaw, the Roger and Bess mysteries, and Song of the Spirit** as well as two contemporary romance series, **Morgan's Run and Morgan's Fire!** Three of her nonfiction titles have been published by Heinemann and she has published numerous articles in the field of literacy education. Lee is a professor emeritus at a small New England liberal arts college where she taught reading and writing pedagogy. Her research, which is ongoing, focuses on mindfulness and connections to reading and writing.

Lee has lived in southern California (loved those Laguna nights), Chapel Hill, North Carolina, and various spots in Massachusetts and Rhode Island. Currently, she resides on the river, where she canoes and swims daily. She is the mother of two grown sons, Ransom and Winward, and spends lots of time with them, their beautiful wives, Alexandra, and Stephanie, and her five extraordinary grandchildren, Abigail, Ava, Camille, Benjamin, and Teddy. When not teaching or writing (both of which she loves), Lee's passions revolve around family, yoga (Kripalu is a second home), swimming, canoeing, gardening, and walking.

Lee loves to hear from readers. Visit her website *http://www.mleep-rescott.com/* and on Facebook *https://www.facebook.com/pages/M-Lee-Prescott/883010881714516*. Her email is *mleeprescott@gmail.com*.